PRAISE FOR SUE DENVER'S WEREWOLF P.I. SERIES

"By the end of [*Werewolf for Hire*] I didn't know if I wanted to scream, hit things, or cry because I already want the next book in the series."

— *THE INTERNATIONAL REVIEW OF BOOKS*

"Sue Denver has written a fascinating character in Sara. She reminds me of Jane Yellowrock from Faith Hunter's series, and in all the right ways: strong, aloof, in control of herself (until she isn't), and mysterious."

— MJ SILVERSMITH, *DISCOVERY*

"Riveting, thought-provoking mysteries that go one step beyond the usual whodunit (or, who will do it) scenarios.

— *MIDWEST BOOK REVIEW*

AMBUSHED IN ALASKA

SARA FLORES, WEREWOLF P.I.

SUE DENVER

CHAPTER ONE

Sara

I was sitting in a recliner with my wolf-dog Skidi, listening to old Patsy Cline heartbreak songs, when I just barely heard a rifle shot.

My cabin was small, one room, and super-insulated to keep out 40-degree-below-zero cold, so it should have kept out the sound. Except that I have extraordinary hearing.

Skidi's ears were standing at attention and oriented to the west, which is where I thought it came from.

Yep — it was a rifle. That was a big problem.

My cabin is in the middle of nowhere Alaska, surrounded by more nowhere. There's not a road within 40 miles of here, so the only firearm I should ever hear was my own.

Who am I? My name is Sara Flores and I'm a 5' 7", 30-something, with shaggy, dark hair. What you most need to know about me is that I'm both a private investigator and a werewolf.

The werewolf part happened because a Lupiti shaman friend of mine on his deathbed transformed me four years ago. He died without telling me a damn thing about my new condition. I've come to believe he was the last descendant of Plains Indian tribes who carried this gene, virus, whatever.

I sometimes believe that I'm the last werewolf in the world. Nobody today believes they ever existed.

As for the private eye part, I wanted to do something good with my new abilities. My company, Last Chance Investigations, specializes in rescuing people targeted by assholes — usually rich ones. If you had poor assholes after you, a bunch of your friends could maybe get together and go beat the crap out of them. Problem solved.

Now, if you're up against a human trafficking ring or a drug cartel, you've got bigger problems. The kind you might come to me to solve.

In the past two years my team and I have been shot, stabbed, run off the road and kidnapped.

But, hey, we're still here and those bad guys aren't.

Skidi was already whining at the door, when I pulled on my "outside" clothes. It was frustratingly slow, because it included an anorak, padded ski pants, a fur hat, thick mittens, and serious fur-lined boots. I picked the white jacket, not the screaming yellow one as stealth was my goal.

I pulled on a polar-fleece balaclava that covered my head except for my face, then added a form-fitting face mask that covered me from right under the eyes to my neck. It had a built-in breather and heat exchanger that warms the air before it hits your lungs. Snow-blindness goggles went on over that.

Before you call me a wuss, I don't see you stepping outside in this kind of weather.

I wouldn't have needed any of this gear if I'd just transformed into a wolf. But being in that form is not recommended when hunters are around.

Not that any should be here. To discourage adventurous hunters from using a plane or snowmobile to come here, I have clear "No Hunting" signs posted all around my property.

I grabbed my Nosler 21 rifle, loaded with a .375 H&H mag, and my snow shoes and went out the door.

In case you're wondering what I was doing in an isolated cabin, as far from humans as was possible without leaving the planet...

I'd come to Alaska to get away from a man.

The kindest, biggest-hearted man I've ever known, not to mention the best looking. And, by the way, the man I've been in love with for the past three years.

He's also the man who is any day now marrying a "nice, Lupiti woman," so they can have nice Lupiti boy babies, so one of them can follow in his daddy's footsteps and become the tribe's priest when his dad retires.

I've spent the past month desperately wanting to punch someone.

Now I just might get my chance.

Although it was mid-April, the thermometer outside my door said it was currently zero degrees Fahrenheit. I quickly checked the wind, which was coming from the direction of the shot. It was strong enough to swirl the latest dusting of snow, lying on top of a three-foot packed layer. It made that zero degrees feel closer to minus 30.

I gave Skidi the signal to stay with me — a pat on the side of my leg — and a finger-over-the-lips sign to be silent.

We moved about a hundred yards from the cabin, then I stopped and smelled the air. I turned west into the wind and, even with my human nose, I could smell a man. I frowned. Maybe two men.

Skidi and I did not run directly towards the shots because, hey, I'm not an idiot. I needed to know what we were facing. If the men were natives, taking down a moose to feed their family, I wouldn't object.

But if anyone touched one of the wolves here... well... let's just say he better not.

I'd only been up here for a month, but I already understood this land like my own body. I knew where ridges, trees, or tall bushes provide cover, and where you could see for miles. Fortunately the smells came from an area with white spruce and thick underbrush. From there, I'd be able to see better while remaining downwind of the hunters.

We reached the trees then crept through a dense thicket of snow mounds covering shrub birch. We got as close to the hunters as possible while still hidden. Again I inhaled the men's scent and now knew they weren't native. I smelled one of those ultra-expensive men's colognes, with blackcurrant and oak moss in it.

I slithered on the snow-packed ground until I could peek around one of the mounds and see.

Yep, two men. Both of them were tall, at least six feet. That's another sign they likely weren't native. They wore expensive white camouflage snowsuits, white fur hats and orange-fading-to-yellow snow goggles with a big "O" on the side that meant they were Oakley's and cost close to $200 a pair.

They were drinking something out of flasks.

Then I smelled blood.

One of the men moved and I saw an animal lying dead at their feet. The fur was thick and white. The smell told me it was a wolf.

Damnit!

I jerked back, my hands shaking.

I wanted to shoot them both. Badly.

I bought this land and was planning on more to turn it all into a wolf sanctuary. I was going to start on the paperwork once I hit 500 acres.

My clenched finger cramped on the trigger and I had to force myself to remove it. Wolf hunting was legal in Alaska. Hell, you had the right here to seek out wolf dens and shoot the mama, pull out every one of her baby pups and shoot them too. You could massacre the entire family and get patted on the back for it.

Hence the need for a wolf sanctuary.

Skidi kept head-bumping me, so I turned to her. She moved her nose to the trees north of where the two men stood and whined quietly. Her tail swished back and forth. It wasn't wagging. She was distressed.

Frowning, I turned my nose to the direction she indicated and inhaled.

Oh, shit. I stood up.

The snow in front of those trees appeared to be moving by itself. Looking closer I could see white, furry bodies, slunk low to the ground. They flowed from the trees towards the two men, who were standing with their backs to the approaching wolves.

It was a whole pack of them. Eight no nine. Creeping closer and closer. This was not normal behavior for wolves.

I gasped and held my breath, scared for the wolves.

The first of them were 10 feet from the men and closing when a large, light-gray wolf came out from the trees and howled.

The men startled and began to turn, bringing their rifles around.

As if the howl were a signal, the white wolves leapt to their feet and flew at the two men, knocking them down. One of the rifles fired, but I didn't see a wolf falter.

He'd missed!

A cacophony of snarling followed as nine wolves made the kills, then shoved each other out of the way to grab the best bites of meat. Both men struggled only briefly. Bright red splattered the snow as their jugulars were ripped open.

I winced, but a part of me felt the men had earned it by killing one of their pack.

So sue me — it felt good to see the underdogs win once.

It's just... wolves don't do this. There have been only two humans killed by wolves in the last 20 years, and those wolves were probably defending themselves.

Wolves have survived despite all the human hatred they've faced by not being stupid. They run from us, if they are given the chance.

So... how could this be?

Skidi nosed me, urgently. I turned to where she looked. I'd forgotten about the huge gray wolf that had howled, almost as if he were signaling the attack. Now he was lying on his back in the snow, a pool of blood over his chest.

I fell to my knees. Two wolves were dead. On my land, which was supposed to protect them.

I looked at Skidi, who was quivering. Why was she...?

The wind carried the dead wolf's smell to me. It was... unusual. It was... almost... human?

I saw the wolf's body jerk and twist then... change.

A naked human man lay on the snow. Unmoving.

Holy shit!

With no thought at all to the pack of wolves, I leapt from cover and ran towards the man — my snow shoes digging in and my heart in my throat.

The man was laying still. He should be getting up. Why wasn't he? He'd been shot in the chest, but that should be no problem for him once he transformed. I always healed instantly.

He could not... I refused to believe... he just *couldn't* be dead.

Fear squeezed my lungs until I was gasping air.

I fell to the snow beside him. No bullet wound marked his chest. He looked healed and yet he lay there. I checked, and he had a pulse, although it was slow. His chest moved as he breathed.

I looked up and startled. Without a sound, his wolf pack had moved to surround us. Their nostrils flared as they inhaled my scent.

Their red muzzles tilted quizzically at me.

I grabbed Skidi and pulled her closer to me, hoping to protect her.

They smelled like natural wolves, but still I said, "Are you... like him?" My eyes moved from wolf to wolf. "Can you help him?"

They showed no signs of understanding my question.

Instead, one by one, they stuck their noses under one of my arms and inhaled. Yes, even through all the clothes they could smell me. Wolf noses are that good.

They had to sense the wolf in me. Maybe they recognized me as someone with the same difference as this man.

The male and female wolves closest to me turned their heads and retreated into the trees. The others followed. The whole pack vanished into the bushes as though they were never here, leaving me and Skidi with the unconscious man. And the remains of the two shooters, which I would have to come back for. Not for their body parts — they'd be feeding the predators around here — but the clothing and rifles would need to disappear.

It would take us maybe a half hour to drag him back to my cabin. His body temperature would be hotter than a human's, but still... that's a long time to be naked in this ice-box landscape.

He had almost no facial or body hair, except for his head which sported a long mess of all-white hair. It suited his face, which was aged with deep grooves, and fit the slack skin over his well-muscled body.

I'd believed the werewolf gene, virus, whatever had its last gasp among Native Americans in the late 1800s. Although... Europe used to be a hotbed of werewolf rumors....

I stopped myself. I wasn't going to solve that question now. Probably never.

He'd been a huge wolf, but as a human he wasn't any taller than me. I stripped off my clothes and dressed him in them. I was most worried about his hands and feet which I carefully covered.

I called up my change to wolf, which is surprisingly simple as I only have to will it. Changing back to human requires eating meat.

Blinding pain? That comes either way.

I always take a big breath and grit my teeth and remind myself it only lasts one minute. But you'd be surprised how much agony you can fit into 60 seconds.

First my face elongates and new teeth break through my gums. My head feels like it's being squished in a vise and my midsection might as well have been run over by a truck. My skin burns as fur comes pouring out and my hands and feet feel like someone took a mallet to them.

Then, about 30 seconds in, it gets much, much worse. That's when my spine cracks to bend the opposite direction and my lungs can't pull in air. I would scream in agony at this point except my voice box is changing and no sounds can escape.

At least, thank god, all those myths were wrong — I don't need a moon to transform. It's just less painful at the first if I'm moon drunk. Nothing eases the last.

For the slog back to the cabin, Skidi and I each grabbed an arm in our jaws and together we dragged him across the ice.

The entire trip back, my head kept screaming, "I am not alone."

He had to survive.

CHAPTER TWO

Mason

Mason Spencer felt like a coward.

He'd been in Anchorage, Alaska, for six days and he still hadn't walked into the Reindeer Bar to see Emma Traboldt. Here he was, sitting in his rental car across the street from the bar for the second night, too damn scared to make his move.

He wanted to give up and leave town, except his mom would ask him what happened. He couldn't tell her that he didn't even try.

It was all his mom's fault, really. She scared the crap out of him and dad when she got thyroid cancer, then took ruthless advantage of his fears — getting him to agree to date three "nice Lupiti girls" she'd picked out for him. Right before she went under the knife.

She ignored his protest that he was only 22.

He would have agreed to anything right then.

Thank god the operation turned out pretty well. She had a 77% chance of being cancer free after five years.

But the nice Lupiti girls had been a pain in the ass. He'd felt no connection with any of them. When he told his mom that, she'd asked him if any girl ever sparked for him. For some reason, he'd thought about Emma, a girl he'd taken some computer classes with, when he was in college.

If his mom hadn't been lying there in the hospital bed, looking so fragile, with black circles under her eyes... Well, if it weren't for that he would have been smart enough to keep his damn mouth shut instead of blabbing about Emma.

Once mom got her name out of him, she wouldn't listen to reason. He'd never even dated the girl. She probably just thought about him as a friend. If that. And she was taken. She'd left town with another man and moved to Alaska.

But mom said maybe she'd changed her mind. Maybe she'd broken up with the guy. Next thing Mason knew, he was making plans to come up here and find out. Thinking it was a great idea.

Until he got here and found she was living in a house owned by the man she left with. They weren't married — Mason had double-checked that. But she was still with the guy.

Mason dropped his head, sighed deeply, and rubbed his eyes with his palms. He should just leave.

But maybe he'd regret it forever?

The thing was, he could actually talk to Emma. Tell her some of his computer work stuff without her eyes glazing over. And when she talked to him, well... it was interesting. She never made him want to puncture his eardrums so he didn't have to hear even one more inane, worthless word.

And he wanted her. He'd wanted her so badly in college that he'd lose the ability to talk. She probably thought he was weird, just staring at her for hours at a time.

Oh hell.

He shook his head and imagined what his business partner, Sara Flores, would say if she could see him now. She'd probably slap him on the back and say something like, "Buck up, kiddo. You survived a guy trying to shoot you point blank. How bad could this be compared to that?"

Maybe he should just go visit Sara instead. Hell, her cabin couldn't be that far from here. He rolled his eyes. The grief she would give him...

He sighed, then forced himself to open the car door.

He frowned at the overcast sky. It'd been gloomy the entire week he'd been here in Anchorage. How could you live in a place without the sun? He scowled at the frigid 10 degree weather, grabbed the hat and gloves he'd had to buy here and shoved them on.

Afraid of slipping on the packed snow — really ice — that covered everything, he minced towards the bar door. He wondered if they had sidewalks or paved parking under the snow in Alaska. Why bother if you never saw them?

He reached the side of the building, then paused. He hoped he looked okay. His long, brown hair was pulled back at his nape and hung halfway down his back. He smoothed it back and re-tied the cord holding it. Being only half Lupiti, his hair had some curl in it which sometimes made it stick out on the sides instead of lying flat.

The bar looked like a dump from the outside. It was a box with concrete walls stamped somehow to pretend to be brick. There was only one window, which you couldn't see in. It had a neon sign on the top saying "Reindeer Bar" that showed a big mug of beer and a billboard advertising "Budweiser on Draft $4.00."

But it was much bigger inside. Mason had seen online pictures and it was large enough to fit 200 people. Maybe Alaskans did all their living inside buildings so they paid no attention to the outside.

He forced himself to grab the door handle, push it, and walk inside. The noise hit him like a punch to the gut. Blaring music, clanging pin ball machines and people yelling so the person next to them could hear what they said.

From the online pictures, he'd planned where he would sit — at the back of the bar where he could see the whole place at once. Mason looked for possible cameras and mikes, as he always did in a new place. He saw five on the ceiling, hidden only in that they were black as was the ceiling. One was pointed right at him.

He felt uneasy and he thought it was more than just seeing Emma again. He pulled out his phone and texted his and Sara's operations manager, Judy Street. She was traveling in an RV to Dollywood with a new boyfriend, but she'd get the message eventually.

> I just went into the Reindeer Bar in Anchorage
> - in case I'm never seen again.

He hit send, then reconsidered. He added a second text.

> Just joking. Probably.

Judy was the smartest hire that he and his partner Sara had ever made. The woman was a logistics genius. If he really did disappear, she'd make sure Sara knew and she'd figure out how to find him.

Mason looked up and saw Emma across the room, coming out from a door marked "private." Their eyes met and Emma looked... well....

His body reacted to her even stronger — even worse — than before. Looking at her made him feel like somebody had a hand around his heart and was squeezing it so hard it couldn't beat.

Her straw-colored hair was pulled back in a ponytail instead of framing her face like he preferred. Her blue-ice eyes were as sharp as ever, stabbing into him.

But now they were surrounded by dark shadows. She looked tired, and, just for a second when she first saw him, she looked horrified. Even frightened.

He shouldn't have come here.

She blanked out her face, making it expressionless, and turned away from him. Strolling to the bar, she talked to the man working there, then moved to a table with an older couple and took their order.

She did not look at him.

He picked up his phone. He was about to stand, to leave, when she walked towards him. She stopped in exactly the spot where her back was to the camera facing his table.

"Do not act like you know me," she hissed.

Loudly, she said, "What'll ya have, hon?"

"A Bud draft."

"Coming up." She turned and moved to the bar.

Mason considered his options. He pulled out one of his business cards that had just two lines on it — "Last Chance Investigations" and the phone number.

Emma came back with his beer, moving close to him as she put it on the table. She looked down at the table and saw the card with his phone written on it. She gave a tiny nod and whispered into his ear so softly he almost couldn't hear it, "You're just a jerk coming onto me. I'll call you in a day or two at that number."

She picked up his card and stuffed it into his own pocket. She said in a normal voice, "You give your phone number to somebody who cares, sweetie. I'm taken."

She turned and walked away.

Mason was sure his face was beet-red and he hated it. He was so screwed.

He sat there, watching her, then realized he wasn't playing the role she wanted him to play. He forced himself to shrug as though it didn't really matter. He grabbed his phone and started flipping through screens, oblivious to what he saw.

He could feel his heart racing.

He suddenly remembered the beer. It was supposed to be why he came in here. He picked up the weighty stein and drank. He wondered if he threw it at a wall would the very thick glass shatter?

He looked at the door she'd gone into. He suspected she wasn't coming back out while he was here. He forced himself to drink the rest of the beer even though his stomach was cramping and he worried the beer would come right back up.

He was pretty sure a man who came into a bar for a drink and just got snubbed by a potential pick-up, would still finish the beer.

If anyone was watching.

He was out the door and halfway to his rental car when he had to turn aside. The beer came rushing back up, spewing out of him with unexpected force. He watched it as the heat of it melted through the ice and sank.

The taste. The smell. He held his stomach trying to prevent more vomit.

He leaned weakly against his car. He might never drink another beer in his life. It wouldn't be a hardship. He didn't like alcohol, especially what it did to his brain. When he drank, he could feel it sliding up inside there — messing with his synapses so they started to misfire.

His brain was the only weapon he had in this crazy world. When he felt it slow down, it panicked him. Made him feel vulnerable.

When he was sure he had nothing more to throw up, he wiped his mouth on his shirt, then got into the car. As he drove away, he ran the entire scene back through his mind. There was something he'd missed...

What?

Then he saw it.

She had looked at his card to memorize the number, but she'd reacted to something. It could only be the name of his company, Last Chance Investigations. Something about the name jolted her — just for a second.

She was in some kind of trouble. Mason nodded. She had better let him help her.

He couldn't wait to get back to his room. To hell with her privacy — he was about to dig deeper into her life than anyone had ever gone before.

But... the entire drive back, he kept seeing her... the blonde hair he wanted to pull out of that pony tail, that button nose that looked like it was supposed to have freckles spread across it, her Midwestern cheerleader look. Her body.

He thought he'd forgotten her. But he wanted her now more than ever.

Which should have been impossible.

CHAPTER THREE

Mason

Mason rose from the torturously designed motel room chair and stretched his body. He looked at his watch and scowled. He'd spent ten straight hours sitting there — nothing really compared to the two- and three-day sessions he'd spend at home. He missed his Aeron chair. He already had a cramp in his back.

He also missed his home computer setup back in Pennsylvania, what Sara called his "Command Central."

It had been almost 24 hours, but Emma hadn't called him yet. Meanwhile, he'd found next to nothing online about her for the two years since he last saw her — just that she'd been working at the bar for a year now and she made a low salary.

He and Emma had both killed their social media accounts in college after seeing what a hacker could learn from them. She hadn't restarted any of hers in the two years since she'd graduated.

He couldn't find what he most wanted to know: why a woman who excelled in both computer science and then economics was waiting tables in a bar.

He had more luck with Gerald Bjorkman, the man who took her

away to Alaska after graduation. Bjorkman, it turned out, was the managing partner and 20% owner of the Reindeer Bar. The other 80% was owned by Martes Empresas S.A., a holding company based in the Bahamas.

Wasn't that interesting? Mason had learned a lot over the past two years while hacking off-shore holding companies. One thing for sure, they were used by very rich men with something to hide. Not by some upper-middle-class nobody like Bjorkman.

The man was 31, seven years older than Emma. He didn't have a criminal record — well, he couldn't have one or he couldn't be an owner in the bar. At least, Mason didn't think so... something to check on. Bjorkman did have a sealed juvie record he'd have to get his hands on.

Mason's phone rang. The ringtone, a classic-rock tune named *Money (That's What I Want)*, told him the call was to his official business number.

Was it Emma?

"Hello, Mase," she said. "Can you come see me now? I'm at a cafe called Kitty's which is about 10 blocks from the bar."

"I can be there in about an hour," he said, trying not to sound desperate.

"An hour? Where are you staying?"

"I need a half hour to finish this thing I'm in the middle of. For a client. It's urgent."

She was silent for a few seconds, then she said, "Well... I'll try but I don't know if I can stay here that long. I'd be missed. Come as soon as you can."

She hung up.

So much for playing hard-to-get. He needed to have enough time to really talk with her.

He started to close his computer, then hesitated. He took an extra two minutes to post all his research to his company's drop box.

Driving in his rental Trailblazer, Mason called Sara. It went straight to voice mail, so he left a message saying he was just checking in.

He caught himself tapping his fingers on the steering wheel, as he sat at yet another stoplight. To stop his brain churning, he called

Connor Rockwood. Connor, Judy, Sara and he were the sole members of their investigations team. Connor was an executive bodyguard and former Special Forces operative.

"What's all this stuff you just sent me?" Connor asked, before Mason could even say hello.

"Me being paranoid," Mason said. "I'm driving to see this girl I knew from college, but something has me worried."

"Way to pick 'em! Maybe you should stick with the girls your mom found for you."

"Very funny. Not." Mason heard voices over the phone. "Where are you?"

"At Lillian's shooting range. Not everyone took off for vacation, like the three of you did."

"Connor, you told me once that if I ever asked myself if I might be in trouble I was already neck deep in shit."

Silence, then Connor said, "What are the signs?"

"I walk into the bar where she works, and there's a ridiculous number of cameras inside. She's all antsy and wants to pretend she doesn't know me. Then she calls me to meet her but doesn't give me enough time to do anything but drive. I mean, it could just be the guy she's with is crazy jealous..."

"Want me to come up there?"

"No, I'm sure I'm overreacting." He pulled into the larger-than-expected parking space for the cafe. There had to be at least 25 cars parked on the dirty snow and ice.

"I'll call you later," he said, then opened the restaurant door and good smells rushed into his nose. It made his stomach growl. Hot coffee, bacon, eggs, sweet rolls — the aromas wafted over him like a caress. He thought he might even be drooling, like Pavlov's dogs.

He saw Emma sitting at a table near the back of the room, by the exit. He looked up and saw she'd seated herself with her back to a camera. He walked over and sat down, facing the camera.

She smiled at him without it reaching her eyes. "You came."

"Of course."

They looked at each other, then she looked down at her coffee.

"Sorry," he said. "I'm starving." He looked for a waitress and waved her over, then placed his order for "Steak, eggs, and lots of black coffee."

When the waitress left, Emma watched her go. She leaned forward and said, "So, Mase. Who's the client you're working for?"

He wrinkled his brow, confused. "Nobody."

She raised an eyebrow at him.

"Really. We closed a case four weeks ago and I'm taking some vacation time."

"And you just happened to stop in Anchorage?"

"You think I'm investigating you?"

Her face froze.

"Why?" he asked.

"Your card said you're private investigators."

"Emma, it's a company. I'm the cyber guy. We have other people to do the boots-on-the-ground."

"Then why are you here?"

Mason looked at her. Maybe they'd talk a little more and he'd go home to Pennsylvania and mope about her for the rest of his life.

No. If this was his one chance, he had to take it.

"I came here to see if you were getting tired of Gerry."

Her eyes grew very big, right before she closed them.

"Oh, Mase," she said, without opening her eyes. "You always did have the world's worst sense of timing."

He reached across the table and put his hand on hers. "Are you in trouble? Can I help?"

She pulled her hand away and opened her ice-blue eyes, staring into his.

"You have to get out of town," she said, her voice as soft as a whisper. "Now. Go back to the hotel, pack and get the hell away."

Mason frowned and opened his mouth to protest.

"Don't," she hissed. "Leave now or I'll never forgive you." She stood, zipped up her parka, and walked out the door.

Mason sat there. Stunned. Flustered. Frustrated.

What was he supposed to do now? The woman kept screwing with his mind.

He stuffed a gob of eggs in his mouth, fished out $30, put it on the table, then stomped out the door.

He recalled every swear word he could remember in Lupiti and was mumbling them under his breath while he slipped and slid towards his car.

Rage and frustration blinded him until he saw nothing but ice, dirt and his feet. He only noticed the bundled-up man when he moved too close to him.

He opened his mouth to say something when his head exploded in pain and the world went black.

CHAPTER FOUR

Sara

It had been an hour since I'd pulled some sweatpants on the naked and unconscious old man — werewolf! — and laid him on my double bed. I'd also piled blankets on top of him.

Still he slept.

I'd made a pot of venison stew with dehydrated carrots and peas that were now both plump and tasty in the broth. Skidi and I had eaten our fill. I'd thought the smell of it or the green tea I'd brewed would wake the man.

But still he slept.

His face was like one of those sepia-toned prints of Native American chiefs from the 1800's, all craggy and looking as if he were a hundred years old. I couldn't take my eyes off him.

Then the air in the room changed. The man lay there... his eyes were still closed. But his nostrils flared.

I moved back from him, so he wouldn't feel crowded — as far as I could in this tiny cabin — then scooped out a bowl of stew for him and held it forward.

"Eat," I said.

His head turned towards me and his eyes opened. He stared at me and scented the stew. Then he turned his nose more towards me. He inhaled. He frowned then took a deeper breath, his eyes glued to mine.

His eyes next darted to Skidi, and he scented her.

Slowly he sat up. He looked down at the sweat pants he was wearing and his scowl deepened.

His head turned sharply as he searched the cabin. His eyes rested on the door. He was going to run away.

He can't! He might be the only other werewolf on the planet. He could not *run away until he answered a whole bunch of my questions.*

I raised my left hand in a "stop" position and forced my fingers to transform to wolf claws. My hand shrunk into a paw.

"Please don't go," I said, shaking at how much my voice sounded like begging. "Please." With my right hand, I held out the bowl of stew.

He froze, half risen from the bed, and stared at me for what seemed a lifetime. Then he eased back on the bed and nodded at me. He reached for the stew and I gave it to him.

He shoveled a big spoonful into his mouth, then scooped another one before his hand paused partway up.

His eyes widened as he slowed his jaws. He closed his eyes for a second, looking like a man who had just tasted the most delicious ambrosia that existed.

I narrowed my eyes. I know my own cooking, and nobody has ever written poems about it. The best you could say is that I don't screw up the natural ingredients too badly.

One mouthful swallowed, he added another — slowly, savoring every flavor. He looked orgiastic. It was too much. Was he mocking me?

His mouth opened and sounds came out — nothing I could understand. He was making a statement of some kind. I looked at him, but he was focused on the food, not me. He brought another scoop to his mouth and started chewing again.

Oh crap.

"Do you speak English?" I asked.

He said something in return, but I had no clue what it was. I wanted to scream! I had so many questions for him.

He pointed to himself and said something that sounded like "Ski ge ca be."

"Ski ge ca be?" I repeated, trying to match my sounds to his.

He nodded, but he also had the hint of a smile. So my pronunciation was good enough to understand, but I had a funny accent?

I pointed at myself and said, "Sara."

He finished the bowl, licked it clean, then put it down. His hands started making different shapes as if he were talking in sign language.

I didn't know sign language.

I closed my eyes and sighed, a black cloud sucking the air from around me.

But wait!

I raised my hand to stop him, then found my iPhone and set it to record.

"Again," I said, but he just stared at me. I made a circular movement with my hands as if to ask him for more.

My hope almost disappeared before he resumed talking and moving his hands. When he stopped I made the gesture again. He continued talking and signing as I filmed.

I'd recorded about 10 minutes when he stopped and took off the pants I'd put on him. He walked to the door, opened it, and went out.

Deflated, I watched him transform into wolf, then run away.

As I closed the door behind him, I noted it had taken him about one minute to transform — the same amount of time it took me.

I poured myself a cup of the hot green tea I'd made and grabbed Skidi for a needed hug.

I'd been fantasizing about sitting around with another werewolf, hanging out, chewing the fat, discussing life as we know it. Sharing experiences and tips.

Like, "Hey, do you ever need to trim your claws?" or "Does rolling around in poop seem fun to you too?"

Instead, I got an antisocial loner — okay, kinda like I'd been — whose language was unintelligible to me. Somebody up there must be laughing their ass off.

I sighed and put a copy of the video into my drop box and sent it to Judy Street, the logistics queen of our company. I told her to find someone who knows sign language and make them sign a confidentiality agreement, before she had them translate this. I stressed it was absolutely critical that nothing the man said could be repeated. If she didn't trust the translator, then don't get it translated.

For all I know, he was talking about his life as a werewolf — not something I wanted out there. I was also worried about him being recognizable to members of his tribe like Joe White Wolf, the man who had transformed me.

I was putting the phone away when I thought to check for messages. A bunch of them were sitting there, waiting. One from Mason, two from Judy, and three from Connor.

I had turned my phone off. There's no point in running away to Alaska to hide out and sulk about my non-existent love life, if I was just going to chat it up on the phone with friends.

But the number of text messages was excessive. Something was wrong.

Each message I checked said I should call them, but Connor's last one was the most emphatic, and the most like him. It just said:

> Turn on your damn phone and call me. I might
> not answer, because I'll be in the air to
> Anchorage.

What the hell? Why was Connor...? Mason was the only one who should be in Anchorage.

CHAPTER FIVE

Mason

Mason woke up with the worst headache ever.

He moved his hands to his temples and pushed lightly. Maybe his head wouldn't explode if he could hold it together with his hands?

It hurt more than the time his friend Steve had decided they needed to get drunk at college. That headache had made him mostly swear off alcohol. Well... at least until yesterday. Was it yesterday?

Carefully, he opened his eyes.

What the hell?

He was lying on a bed with a ceiling so low that he wouldn't be able to sit up without hitting his head. Seeing nobody, he leaned his head out the opening and saw sliding doors that could close off the bed area. The rest of the room was no more than eight feet by four. The walls were all wood or fake wood and there were three doors.

His stomach twisted as the bed moved a little. He was on a boat.

Was there someone above him?

He slipped out of the bed, holding his head and wincing in pain. There was a top bunk, with nobody on it.

He saw two portholes for the top bunk! He leaned his face into them, but it was night so he only saw fog and lights reflected off water.

He stepped to one of the three doors and tried the handle. It wouldn't move.

One of the other doors was for a small closet with nothing in it. The third one opened into the smallest bathroom he'd ever seen. He could touch all four walls standing in one place, and that included the back wall of a shower he wasn't sure he could turn around in.

Mason took four steps back and sat down on the lower bunk, with his butt in and his head leaning out. He noticed his hands were shaking, so he pressed them into the sides of his head again and leaned out even further, his elbows on his thighs.

"It's not the same," he told himself. "It's not the same."

No, when he was kidnapped almost three years ago, he'd awakened in a bigger room. No metal walls. On solid ground. With a bucket for a toilet. Heck, these were luxury quarters compared to that.

But... they were *on-the-move* quarters.

Crap, how would Sara find him now? She'd rescued him the last time. Saved his life.

Could she find him on a ship? What if it just kept moving? And... her wolf? It would give her no advantage here.

And... Emma? Where was she?

His breath caught in his throat. Was she in on this? Did she set him up?

He refused to believe it.

There was a knock at the locked door, right before it swung in and slapped the back wall.

Handcuffs were tossed on his bed by a man pointing a pistol at him. A man who wasn't covering his face, which was absolutely not a good sign. A man who looked like a football tight end, but with the beginnings of a paunch.

"Put these on," he said.

Mason did nothing.

"I can drag you out or you can walk out. Your choice."

"Some choice." Mason slipped them on, and let the ratchet catch at the loosest setting.

The man nodded back over his shoulder and another man came in, equally tall but more wiry, less bulky. He moved to Mason's side, so his partner could keep the gun on him. He grabbed Mason's wrists and squeezed the ratchets so they clamped down tight on his wrists.

"Ow!"

"Suck it up," the new guy said. "Things could get a *lot* worse."

They walked him down a long wood-paneled hallway with the wiry guy in front, the pistol-carrying linebacker behind. They took him through a door to a utilitarian stairway — most likely a stairway for staff only. He went up two flights before they stopped him, one step from the top landing.

Wiry guy pulled a hood from his jacket and plopped it down over Mason's head so he couldn't see anything.

Both his arms were grabbed, and he was pulled up the last stair, then through a door he heard open. Blindly he walked with one man on either side of him.

They took him through another door, then — suddenly — he could smell the ocean.

He heard, "Stop."

Both men let go of his arms, then one grabbed his belt from behind.

The front man said, "There's a larger than normal step up right in front of you."

Mason raised a foot high then carefully put it down.

"Go up the step and stop."

Mason did.

"Now, you've got about four paces at level ground before you're going to have three steps going down."

Mason walked slowly, then stopped. His foot came out and cautiously felt for ground that wasn't there."

"It's a normal step down."

Mason took it, then three more steps. He believed he was going down into something small, because his shoulders twitched as if the walls were closing in on each side.

Were they going to bury him in a pit? No — I'm on a boat. I'm okay.

He took two steps forward and felt queasy. The floor was moving under his feet. A smaller boat?

He was told to turn around and sit down. He put out his elbows and hit a wall right behind where he was supposed to sit.

Once seated, they locked his cuffed wrists to an arm of his chair. One of the men sat on his right. Mason moved a shoulder to his left and hit another wall. He heard the second man sit down in front of him.

There was a door-closing noise, then a suction sound — a hatch closing? An engine started and his seat moved under him. The smaller boat must be detaching.

Soon he felt himself slightly pushed back in his chair. They were moving. But... then his chair tipped slightly forward.

He must be imagining it.

No, he wasn't.

They were going down, as well as forward. When his ears popped, he knew for sure.

He was in a submarine — a tiny one.

How in the hell would Sara ever find him now?

CHAPTER SIX

Sara

I met with the whole team, except for Mason, the next day in Anchorage. Connor had booked Judy and me each a room on the same floor as his at the Captain Cook hotel.

Today Connor looked like an upscale mountain man, but he could also appear as a slick executive bodyguard, which he'd been the last few years before joining us. At 6' 4" and about 240 pounds, he could intimidate bad guys with just a look. That often came in handy.

Thanks to my wolf, I might be as strong as Connor, although I had never put it to the test. But nobody was intimidated by my looks.

Why hadn't I tested myself against him? Because he knew how tough women in the military were. If I were a lot stronger than them, he'd never stop trying to find out why. As of now, only Mason and my now-ex boyfriend Bill knew my secret — two people too many in my opinion.

Judy was, well, Judy. On the surface, she is the sweetest thing, around 50-something, although I'd never dare to ask what the "something" is. She's small, with pixie-cut grey hair that always looks like she just got out of bed. She wears girlie clothes that show off her great figure and more makeup than anyone I know — and it all looks good on her. She flirts with every man she meets, and they flirt back.

In sum, she looks like the kind of woman I should never, ever hire: a victim just waiting to happen for the dangerous men and situations I'm always getting into. Yet, I owe her my life. One time she found me an escape helicopter in Mexico and in less than two hours she had me flying away from more trouble than I could handle.

Before we said anything other than our greetings, I needed to make sure there weren't any listening devices. Mason had shown me how to search my Tulsa office, so I'd ordered the equipment I needed overnighted to me here.

Judy fluffed her hair while watching me then said, "I do appreciate y'all's caution, but isn't this just the teensiest bit overkill?"

Connor shook his head. "I don't think so. Mason's not the only one missing. The woman he came up here to see — Emma Traboldt — supposedly quit her job yesterday, right after Mason went missing. She told the girls who worked with her at the Reindeer Bar that she was going off with a friend to spend the next two months as ski bums."

"Maybe he's with her," Judy said. "I checked his hotel room and he didn't leave much behind. His wallet was gone along with his kit bag and computer equipment. I think some clothes, too. It looks like he went away for a couple of days but planned to return."

She pulled some receipts out of a briefcase and laid one on the table, pointing at it. "And check this out. He fully equipped himself for a ski trip. Clothes, skis, boots. He blew $1,900 on his credit card and none of it was in his room."

I picked up the receipt, more worried than I'd been before.

"Just one problem with this," I told them. "Mason doesn't ski. I teased him about it once, living in Pennsylvania as he does. He told me he was too smart to risk his body for thrills. He said he got all the adrenaline rush he needed from hacking."

"What about the girl's live-in boyfriend?" I asked Connor.

"It's Bjorkman and he's missing too. The bar says he's out for three days 'looking at properties,' whatever that means."

I looked at each of them. "Other than his research dump to all of us, Mason left me nothing except a phone message saying he was 'checking in.' What have you two got?"

Connor said, "He told me he was worried he was stepping into something dangerous, but he didn't know why he felt that way."

Judy opened her briefcase again and handed out a pack of papers to me and Connor. "These are copies of the research he posted. I tried to reach him two hours later and got no response. So it was right before he went missing."

Connor and I paged through the pages, hoping to spot something new. Mason had done a lot of research on Gerald Bjorkman, Emma's love interest for the past two and a half years. He owned a house in Anchorage and some property up near Fairbanks, about 50 miles from mine. He also owned a tiny 20% of the Reindeer Bar.

Mason had also broken into Emma's cloud storage. She was apparently doing the books for the bar. She'd found four women who got irregular, very high payments from the place. Ten thousand dollars for one. Fifteen thousand for another. None of the women were day-to-day employees of the bar.

Emma had also found the exact amount of each payment to every one of the women was returned to the bar at the end of the same month. The return checks were from a company that doesn't seem to exist — no website, no local address. Gerry had booked them as "Consulting Income."

Lastly, Mason had found the holding company that owned the other 80% of Bjorkman's bar— a Martes Empresas, based in the Bahamas.

"Doesn't that sound unusual to y'all?" asked Judy. "A blind corporation in the Bahamas owning almost all of a honkey-tonk bar in Anchorage?"

"Sounds unusual to me," Connor said.

"Me too," I said. "And that raises a very big problem. How are we going to find Mason when he's the only one in this team with hacking ability? Finding someone like this was *his* job."

We all sat there, letting that sink in.

"Well...," said Judy. "We can all do research. I can find out what's publicly available on Martes Empresas. But, I don't know how to find hidden owners of blind corporations."

"What else do we need?" Connor asked.

I blew out a breath of air. "We need someone to break into security cameras and find where Mason was when he got taken. We need to hack into his rental company and see all the places where his car stopped. We need to break into cameras, near where his car last was, and use facial recognition to find what happened to him."

I turned to Connor. "You know anyone who can do that?"

He shook his head. "Last time I needed that kind of intel, it came from the DIA, the Defense Intelligence Agency, or the CIA." He smirked. "I don't think any of them will help us."

"Our former clients?" I asked Judy. "Any of them have these skills?"

She thought about it, then shook her head. "When they volunteered to help us any way they could as thanks, I made some notes. None of them have hacking computer skills. The only one with money — that Doug Ramsey that car dealer in Tulsa — has a computer guy, but one with e-marketing skills, not what we need."

Judy stared at me. "We are so screwed."

We were all quiet. I felt my blood pressure rise. We *had* to find Mason.

"Well, hell," Connor said, "Mason can't be the only hacker in the world."

"No..." said Judy, "but there's a big trust issue with anyone else."

I remembered something. Someone. "Maybe not, but..."

I looked at Judy. "See if you can find what happened to a guy named Steve Callahan. He was in the computer science program at Lock Haven University, in Pennsylvania. Probably graduated the same year as Mason. If not, it would have been no more than a year earlier or later. If you can, get us on a plane to visit him. You and me."

"Let him know we're coming?"

I shook my head. "No. Better to see where he's at first, then surprise him."

I turned to Connor. "You take Bjorkman. Use what Mason found here," I nodded at the paperwork, "and come up with some story that lets you go undercover. Join any group he hangs out with. Get yourself embedded, then see if he shows up in three days. If not, you'll have a better idea of who the players are."

Connor nodded. "I should search his house too. But he may have a silent alarm. Damnit. I never realized just how dependent we are on Mason."

"Join the club."

I got up and walked to the balcony door and went out. I rested my arms on the railing and stared at Point MacKenzie across the Cook Inlet. It was April 16th, but everything was still white. The waterway looked like it was covered in white lily pads made of ice — some quite large, but most flat, ovoid circles in what little water could be seen.

I shivered. It all looked so cold and empty.

Already I missed Mason. And my dog Skidi.

I'd had just enough time to put her on a charter plane back to Tulsa where she could enjoy her favorite place: Doggie Day Care and Amusement Park. The owner would pick her up at the airport and look after her. He'd done it before. Investing in upgrades for his business had brought me more than a couple of very necessary perks.

I had a flash of annoyance at Judy. She'd brought her cat Lola, who hates my guts, to Anchorage. I wished I could have Skidi here.

I shivered again. Judy had come out on the balcony behind me. She put an arm around my waist and squeezed.

"We'll find Mason," she said.

"Yes, we will," I agreed.

And nobody had better have hurt him.

CHAPTER SEVEN

Sara

Judy and I pulled up in front of a standard-looking family house that was just inside the city limits of State College, Pennsylvania. It was all on one floor, except for a lower-level drive-into basement garage.

"You sure this is it?" I asked her.

"I know it doesn't look like it," she said. "But this place rents for $2,500 a month. A price like that is crazy for the middle of nowhere Pennsylvania."

Steve Callahan had joined Allied Health Services in State College, right after graduation. Today, three years later, Steve had been outsourced by Allied. He still handled their cyber threat assessment, but was also open to new clients, such as his recently added Lycoming Junior College.

"This is just 40 minutes from Mason's place," I said. "You think they stayed in touch?"

"If they were girls they would have. Guys? I don't know."

"Judy," I teased. "Something you don't know about males?"

She raised an eyebrow and used her exaggerated-drawl voice.

"Honey, I know all the important stuff I need to. Anything else is just minutiae."

We walked to the door, me wondering how Steve might have changed in three years.

I'd never met him in person, but Steve had been a scared kid when we talked. The goons that came after Mason, when he'd hacked the wrong computer, had done a number on Steve's face — trying to find out where Mason was. By the time they'd kidnapped Mason, Steve had moved out and was pretty much in hiding.

I'd called Steve because I needed to find Mason fast. I figured if I could find his computer — which the goons had taken — I would probably find Mason nearby.

Steve was terrified, but he'd found the courage to help me, and I was able to find and rescue Mason.

I looked at the change in the two photos of Steve that Judy had found. There was his fat-cheeked college photo and his slimmer, more confident photo for his new company. Did finding that inner courage change his whole self image?

Judy rang the doorbell. A young woman with long, dark-brown hair and a quizzical expression opened the door.

"Yes?"

"Hi sweetie," Judy said, "We're looking for Steve Callahan's offices. Is this the right place?"

"Well... yes... but... we don't see anyone here. Let me get you a card." She turned and walked back to a desk situated in what should have been the living room.

Judy and I walked into the house after her.

She turned, with a card for us, but her eyebrows shot up in alarm. "You can't come in here. He doesn't see anyone here." She shoved the card at us. "You'll have to call and set up an appointment then he'll come to your office."

I moved to a sofa in the room and sat down. "He'll see us. He did a job for me three years ago and I want to hire him again, this time for money." I pulled out our Last Chance Investigations card and held it out to her.

Reluctantly, she took it from me. She looked flustered, her pale white skin a rosy pink. She wanted us out of the house but wasn't stupid enough to try pulling me up, off the chair.

Judy put an arm on hers. "Sweetie, he'll see us. It's about his friend Mason." She smiled and nodded at the girl, then sat down beside me.

The girl just stood there. "You'd better go get him," Judy said, shooing her with her hand.

The girl turned and practically ran out of the room.

"So," I said to Judy, "you think she's doing Steve?"

"Bet on it."

The man who came into the room looked very much like his new company photo. Oh, his eyes were still too close together and his nose too big for good looks, but he'd lost some weight and was wearing a quality shirt and pants.

More importantly, he looked me in the eyes and stood his ground. "What job did I do for you before?"

"You found Mason's computer for me, so I could find him."

"You're the woman?"

I nodded.

"And it's about him again?"

I nodded.

"Come back to my office." He turned and Judy and I followed.

The room we went to had more computers than I'd ever seen in one office, but then I'd never been to Mason's "Command Central." We sat across from Steve's semi-circular desk which had three laptops on it, while along the wall behind him there was ten feet of table space with at least eight more computers.

Steve sat behind the desk and leaned back in his executive chair staring at me. "I'd always wondered what you looked like. I mean, Mason told me, but there's a big difference between description and seeing someone with your own eyes.

I smiled.

"Doing that job for you... it changed me."

When he didn't add anything else, I said, "I thought it might. You were very brave."

He grinned. If it was a little bit smug, I didn't begrudge him. He'd earned it.

"You're here about Mason now?"

"We're pretty sure he's been kidnapped."

"What, again?" Steve laughed. When he saw our somber faces, his smile evaporated. "Sorry. It's just..."

"It would be funny, you're right. But we're too worried about him. Has he told you about our business?"

"I know you find and rescue missing people, and you go up against some very bad men. I know you broke that female trafficking ring run by that casino guy."

"We've been very successful, but a large part of our success was due to Mason. Now that we need him most, we don't have him."

The girl popped her head into the room. "I'm sorry, Mr. Callahan, but it's time for that video conference."

I bit my lip to keep from grinning. The girl wasn't very good at it, but she was trying to give Steve an out.

He smiled at her. "It's okay, Suzie. They work with my friend Mason. We're all good."

She stared hard at him, but he grinned and she left.

"We can pay you. Whatever you want."

"I know."

Huh? Just how much has Mason told him?

"The problem is," he said, "I'm not as good as Mason. I mean, I'm very good. But Mason... he'd see openings nobody else could. I can't get into some of the databases that I know he's been in."

"Our problem right now is finding traffic or other video footage that will show who took him. We also need to find out who's behind a holding company in the Bahamas named Martes Empresas. And we need to dig deeper into Emma Trabolt, because Mason found nothing thus far."

"You think she's involved?"

"He went to Anchorage to see if she was still happy with Gerald Bjorkman. Mason dug into him. We can give you a copy of what he found. But there's not much more on him other than the oddity of a Bahamas company owning 80% of his bar."

I looked at Steve. "You knew Emma?"

He nodded.

"Did she seem like the kind of girl who'd be happy enough with a man to wait tables at a bar for three years? After graduating with a double major in computer science and economics? I'm thinking we must have missed something."

Steve shook his head. "You're asking the wrong person." He gave a quick glance at the door to make sure Suzie wasn't there. "Why women do what they do is still pretty much a mystery to me."

I smiled.

Judy said, "Don't you worry about it, sweetie. We women, well... we all work very hard to keep men confused."

I rolled my eyes. "What I'm trying to say is that thus far, this job doesn't look as complex as some of the ones we've done. Can you tap into traffic footage?"

"Probably."

"Uncover ownership of Bahamas-incorporated companies?"

"Definitely. And I can dig into Emma. I do a lot of background investigations."

"Excellent!" I said. "And you have one very big advantage, as far as working with me."

He cocked his head.

"You've proven yourself trustworthy."

His mouth tightened. "Okay, he said. "What do we do?"

I looked around. "Do you have another office Judy could use?"

"Judy?"

"We need answers yesterday. Nobody is better at research than her, if it doesn't require hacking. She can free you up to work on the hard stuff. And if she hits a snag, she'll be able to point you to who has the info and what she needs to uncover.

"Also, she knows what Connor and I can do, and she'll recognize what's important and what isn't. If you two find a trail that requires someone on the ground, she can get Connor or me on it in seconds.

Steve and I both turned to Judy.

She nodded at Steve and said, "The sooner we start the faster we find Mason."

Judy turned to me. "Shoo. Drive back to the airport. I'll call you with plane info in a few minutes. If I can get you a charter that's faster, I will."

I smiled. "Consider me shooed."

I nodded at Suzie as I left. I couldn't imagine she would like dealing with the hurricane that is Judy, but she might. Women seemed to fall under Judy's spell as much as men did. It was one of her gifts.

And... yes, I was a little jealous of her ability. But it seemed to require calling someone "hon" or "sugar," and... well... I had to laugh.

I couldn't imagine doing that.

CHAPTER EIGHT

Sara

I'd landed back in Anchorage late that same afternoon, thanks to a charter jet the amazing Judy had managed to hire for me with only an hour's notice.

You might be wondering just where our money was coming from, so we could take charter jets and stay in top hotels. You'd be right to wonder. Every other private investigator I'd met was working hard to make a living and scrimping to get by. It was a favorite job for former cops, and heaven knows we don't pay them anything near what we should, given the risks of their job.

Mason and I figured out how to fund our work on our second case together. We took down a murdering son-of-a-bitch politician in New York City, and by "took down" I meant we permanently removed him from life. Mason had tracked his finances and found a tidy little $2 million dollars that he'd hidden in an offshore account in the Caribbean island of Nevis. We didn't touch his legal money, but helped ourselves to his tax-fraud funds.

It covered the costs on our next two cases, before we had another job with a rich murderer. In that case, we found $5 million hidden in Bogota, Columbia. Our last haul was $14 million.

So we lucked into our "business model." It gives us the funds to take on wealthy assholes, who could bury a poor detective in legal problems, not to mention the army of bad guys they could hire for a more permanent solution.

Besides... we knew how pissed off our "donors" would be that their money was being spent to help the powerless and take down other "superior" assholes like them.

It's our middle-finger salute to men who got off easy being dead.

Judy called me at five that evening, and put Steve on the phone to give me an update.

"Mason's car last stopped at Kitty's Cafe before coming back to the hotel. Kitty's shares a parking lot with Anchorage Bank, and the bank had a camera. I hacked in, but his car was a dead end. It sat at the cafe for three hours after Mason arrived, then a guy in a bulky ski jacket, thick gloves and a fur hat got in and drove it to Mason's hotel, leaving it there. Judy says it wasn't Mason because the walk was wrong. Also, the unknown guy looks to be an inch or two shorter.

"We then looked at all the vehicles that left the cafe not long after Mason arrived. They had to be close enough to the building that Mason, either walking or unconscious, could have gotten into the vehicle or been carried to it without us seeing it due to the camera angle. We only saw full license plate numbers on two of them, but both checked out.

"However, one van in the lot was using a holographic cover over the license plate. That's illegal because it distorts the letters for any traffic camera. That van left about 45 minutes after Mason arrived, but we lost it pretty quickly. Anchorage doesn't have anywhere near the number of traffic cameras most cities do.

"But...?" I was beyond impatient. They wouldn't have wasted my time like this if there wasn't more.

"But," Steve said, "it was a black Mercedes van. They'd blacked out the Mercedes logo on the back, but I could tell by the shape. The Chevy van is rounder on the sides, the Ford van is boxier at the top. It was definitely a Mercedes.

"How many Mercedes vans are there in Alaska?" I asked.

"Their DMV doesn't publish that info," Judy said. "But there can't be that many. There's only one dealership in the state. All told there are 44,000 commercial vehicles here, of which vans are a tiny part and Mercedes an even smaller percent."

Steve jumped in. "I'm using Mason's customized image recognition software — he's lucky he gave me a copy! — and it's searching everywhere for a black van of that shape. We're looking at Anchorage traffic cams as well as cameras at the private airports and piers. If they didn't drive him away, a private plane or boat would be their only option."

"Meanwhile," Judy said, "tell her what else you found."

Steve said, "I peeled back one layer of Martes Empresas. Turns out they also own Schlossen Security, a private company with offices in a number of large U.S. cities including — surprise! — Anchorage.

Judy chimed in. "I wondered why an offshore company would own both a national security company and 80% of a tiny bar in Anchorage. I thought Connor should do a job interview with Schlossen to get on the inside, but he's got another lead that he'd be the best one to follow.

"Connor found Bjorkman belongs to the Joseph Lake Sportsman Club, a hunting and fishing club that is way too rich and exclusive for him. And guess who else belongs to that club?"

"Tell me."

"The guy who runs the Anchorage branch of Schlossen Security. Who is also a member of the same Anchorage Rotary Club that Bjorkman belongs to."

There was a knock on my door. "One second. I think my dinner's here."

Ah, the aroma. There's nothing like a very rare steak and — because this place catered to the rich — green beans and broccoli tempura. Yum!

I took a big bite of the steak and tossed a broccoli floret in my mouth.

"I don't know," I mumbled around the food. "Could it be coincidence?"

I heard Judy ask, "Are you eating *again*?"

"Yes, Judy. I eat three or four times a day."

I heard her whisper, "More like five or six," which she thought I wouldn't hear.

She said, "It could be a coincidence, if it weren't for Bjorkman. No way he belongs in that hunting club. The annual dues are $125,000 and any excursions are on top of that. His bank records show he only cleared $145,000 all of last year."

I thought about it and took another bite.

"Sara?"

"I'm here."

Judy continued, "I figured Connor would be best to look into the hunting club, since the membership is all male, except for spouses. And you could look into Schlossen Security. I booked you an appointment for 10 AM tomorrow. I told them you were thinking about opening an Anchorage office for our expanding business."

"You did, huh?" I shook my head and grinned, then popped in another bite of steak.

"Was I wrong?"

"No, I like it."

"Then you'll *really* like this. I put $150,000 of your money in Connor's bank account and told him to join the hunting club."

I shook my head. "Judy, Judy. I give you an unlimited budget and you exceed it."

"But I... wait... Isn't that a quote about some NFL guy? Cute! But I was right to do it, wasn't I?"

"It's Mason," I said. "We spend whatever we need to find him as fast as we can."

CHAPTER NINE

Sara

So here I was, knocking on Schlossen Security's door for my 10 AM meeting.

I hoped one of our many leads would pay off soon. I needed Mason to be home safe.

Emil Wissen, the owner of Schlossen in Anchorage, had a shock of dark red hair that was all I saw at first. The red wasn't only on top, but was also a bush covering his entire lower face. You couldn't look at him and not think "mountain man."

However, he also had a gold Rollex, a custom-fitted suit and a pair of piercing blue eyes. His shoes gleamed like polished marble, with three straight lines of laces and a small braid across the toe. Judy had shown me something like this when I teased her once about the status brands of clothes she liked. She claimed men paid $3-4 thousand for a pair of these shoes.

Wissen ushered me to a chair in front of his desk, which was made to look like a four-by-six foot slab of wood. The top had swirls of black on dark brown, as if it were cowhide.

The show of wealth seemed, at least to me, over-the-top.

He perched half his ass on the front of the desk, not coincidently towering over me.

"What can Schlossen Security do for you, Ms. Flores?"

I smiled and leaned back in my chair. I even crossed my legs, consciously putting myself in an inferior position for defending myself. I ignored the "threat" of his stance.

Because, hey, when your mouth can turn into a wolf snout in seconds ... I knew he'd lose any part of himself that tried to attack me.

"I have a very small company that has had some rather large success."

"Yes," he said, showing he did his homework. "I read about that casino owner and the sex trafficking ring. Good job."

I nodded. "But with success come bigger problems. Bigger enemies. Bigger threats."

I looked into his eyes. "I like my company the size it is. I don't want to add employees, so I'm considering how much of our security I want to outsource. Bodyguards, certainly, although, how often..." I twisted my hand back and forth to show uncertainty.

"Security for our offices, possibly. Network security, probably not, but that would be up to my partner."

"Mason Spencer, isn't it? I'd like to meet him."

He looked interested, but not overly so. If he was acting, he was good at it.

"Haven't you already met?"

He shook his head. "Never had the pleasure."

I inhaled. My wolf nose detected no apocrine-gland fear stink, which would have told me he was lying.

"Mason's tied up right now." I used those words specifically and inhaled. Again, not even a molecule of odor. "Maybe some other time."

I said, "Your website sounds like you offer full-service security as well as a la carte. True?"

"Yes."

I stood up. I'd learned what little there was to take away from this in-person meet.

"Why don't we try out some a la carte services to see how well we get along. Give me some per diems for bodyguards, along with whatever you charge for extras. And send me a proposal to set up physical security for a new Anchorage office."

"We'll get something to you by Tuesday."

"Excellent."

I extended my hand to him, curious to see what kind of handshake he'd give. It was business firm, not too soft and not too hard. Sort of non-committal, just like the man.

But his eyes... there was a little bit of evaluation showing in their dark, dark blue. More interest than I'd expect for a potential modest-sized client. And it wasn't sexual.

He was wondering how much I knew about something.

CHAPTER TEN

Judy

Judy Street looked around the boxy spare office that she'd been given at Steve's company and wanted to scream.

She'd done everything she could think of to help find Mason. She'd set up Sara with Schlossen Security and Connor with the Joseph Lake Sportsman's Club that Bjorkman belonged to. And Steve was still searching for the black Mercedes van as well as peeling another layer down into the ownership of the Martes Empresas.

Now she had nothing to do.

She pulled Lola onto her lap. Thank goodness for her cat. She missed George and his sweet RV, which was the size and shape of a bus. She missed the RV's electric fireplace and the neat cabinets for everything. She missed sex.

She and Lola had been staying with George at the Pigeon Forge RV Resort when Mason disappeared. They'd only had one day of fun at Dollywood, before she had to leave. George called her an "adrenaline junkie." He was probably right.

Which was exactly her problem now.

She'd spent the last two hours spinning her wheels, trying to think of anything else she could do to help find Mason.

She needed something — anything really — to occupy her mind so it didn't keep wandering to what was happening to Mason.

Then she remembered the video Sara had sent her right as this was hitting the fan. The one of the old man with the sign language. He was also talking while he was signing, but it was a language she'd never heard.

There was something weighty about the guy. Impressive. And something funny about how worried Sara was that someone might learn what he said...

Darn it! Mason was her go-to source for anything Native American.

What if... *oh my*.... What if she contacted Bill Hanalho, Sara's apparently ex-boyfriend? She knew he was some big shot for the Lupiti Nation. She knew Mason trusted him and so did Sara. At least Sara did until last week,when she suddenly left town and all she said was that Bill was getting married.

Obviously not to Sara.

Judy didn't understand the problem. Once, in a moment of girl-bonding, Sara had told her Bill's story. That he had to marry within the tribe to produce sons to carry on the wisdom and traditions of the Lupiti Nation.

As far as she could see, Bill was only doing what he'd always intended to do. What Sara knew he planned to do.

Before she could stop herself, she grabbed her phone and looked up his number — which was listed.

"Is this Bill Hanalho?" she asked.

"Yes?"

"This is Judy Street. I work with Sara Flores and Mason Spencer. I need your advice."

"Did Sara tell you to call?"

"No, and, sweetie, from what I've heard about your forthcoming marriage, I'm pretty sure you're the last person she'd want me to talk to."

There was a long silence. "Then why are you?"

"She sent me a 10 minute video she took of an old Native man talking in mostly sign language. Along with some spoken language I'd never heard. She asked me to get it translated, but under no circumstances can the person who looks at it ever tell anyone what it says."

Judy paused, but Bill said nothing.

"I know she and Mason both trusted you. I was hoping you had ideas about how to do this. Do you know someone you trust who knows American Sign Language?"

"Yes. If that's what it is. If he's really old... it could be Hand Talk instead."

"Hand Talk?"

"P.I.S.L. It stands for Plains Indian Sign Language. Send it to me, and I'll see what I can find."

"Bill, it's critical to her that whatever he's saying is confidential. I don't know why, but...."

"I'll make sure."

"Okay, give me your private email. I'll put it in a secure drop box. And, Bill? Let me know as soon as you know if it's this 'Hand Talk.'"

"I will."

Judy wrote down his email.

"And Bill? Just for the record, I hate you on Sara's behalf."

He snorted, then mumbled, "Join the club."

He hung up.

Judy stared at the phone. *Hand Talk. How interesting...*

She searched for it in her browser and saw quite a few entries. She clicked on a YouTube video that compared ASL to PISL, with one practitioner of each showing the signs for different words. So she could look from one to the other.

She immediately recognized a sign in Hand Talk from Sara's old man in the video. His index fingers had pointed at each other, almost meeting, then both hands rotated 90 degrees so the fingers and thumbs were pointing forward.

That means "tribe." Hmm... maybe she wouldn't need Bill to tell her which sign language it was.

She found a longer YouTube video where a Shoshone man named Willie LeClair showed one sign after another. She put her legs up on the desk and leaned back in the chair. Her hands made the signs along with him.

To talk about the past, LcClair showed the signs for the setting sun, and then brought his right hand forward, as though pushing something back. It meant back into the past.

He also showed the signs for many, many snows ago. He held two fists forward, palms down, and flashed his fingers wide, several times. That was for many. Then he raised both hands, palms still down, and fluttered his fingers as he brought his hands down. Judy could almost see the snow falling.

Interesting how the signs were so intuitive. For anything you could see, you had hand motions. Peaked fingers for mountains. A flat hand cutting across the stomach for hungry.

She bet herself that tomorrow she'd remember half or more of what she learned today. Unlike when she'd tried to grasp Spanish — where the next day she'd forgotten almost everything. After all, there was nothing you could see about a cat that would cause you to call her a "gato." Unlike....

Judy froze. She hit pause on the video. Being here in Pennsylvania was ridiculous. Steve didn't need a babysitter and the action was in Alaska. She could study this sign language there. Or even on a plane there.

Ask Sara?

Why? The woman said she valued initiative. Well, she'd show Sara some.

She grinned and called the charter service she'd found for Sara earlier. Lola was not flying in some unpressurized baggage hold.

She needed maybe an hour to pack up.

She wasn't bored any longer.

CHAPTER ELEVEN

Connor

Connor Rockwood took a sip of his boilermaker and looked around the Joseph Lake Sportsman's Club bar. He was curious to see all that he'd bought after paying an "initiation fee" of $125,000 to join this club. Which didn't include the costs of any hunting or fishing trip he wanted. For example, a 10-day bear-hunting trip would cost another $35,000. Per person.

There were also annual dues, but they were irrelevant. He wouldn't be a member anywhere near that long.

Connor had told Judy what getting in here would cost and she hadn't blinked. She'd wired $150,000 to his bank account overnight.

It was a damn good thing their little P.I. company was rolling in money.

Connor grinned, thinking about where the funds came from. Sara had hired him twice as a contractor, then decided she wanted him to join the team full time. When they'd rescued those girls from a multi-million-dollar sex trafficking ring, Connor was ready to consider it. But he had to know where their money came from. He told Sara he wouldn't join any business funded by groups working against the interests of the United States.

She'd told him that when their company took down rich bad guys, Mason grabbed any money they had hidden offshore. Like the $14 million the head of that trafficking ring had in Caribbean accounts.

The men couldn't object — being as they were now dead.

The result was their little four-person team was funded well enough to go up against pretty much anyone. Heck, they took down the CEO of the multi-billion-dollar KDRP Oil & Gas in their last case.

Connor enjoyed going after the biggest bad guys. He'd grown tired of missions that took down lower-level thugs and let the masterminds escape.

This Joseph Lake Sportsman's Club was full of surprises. For example, the very few personal questions he'd had to answer to join it. Maybe they thought that anyone who could spend this kind of money was automatically the "right" kind of person?

The Club's lodge was in the middle of nowhere, 40 air miles from Anchorage. He'd taken a plane to get here and the views were flat-out spectacular with icy, blinding-white everywhere and mountains as plentiful — and as sharp — as quills on a porcupine.

They reminded him of the peaks in Afghanistan. Treacherous. And cold. There was a reason he was now based in Tulsa, Oklahoma.

The plane landed on the still-frozen Joseph Lake and motored to the club's dock, where employees helped him off the plane. Officially he wanted a look-see and a lunch crafted by the club's supposedly world-famous chef. Then he was flying back to Anchorage.

His real reason was to find out if Gerald Bjorkman, Emma Traboldt, or — best of all — Mason was here.

The data dump from Mason had included Bjorkman's tax returns, where he'd listed his membership in this club as a business expense.

Connor got the "new member" tour, which included all the rooms not currently occupied by members. This place was a rich man's idea of "rustic." Mainly wood, wood, and more wood, with leather chairs and accents.

As a result of the tour, he knew only two guest rooms had current occupants.

It was unlikely anyone staying here would miss lunch, which would be served in a half hour. Connor sank down in one of the bar's dark green overstuffed leather chairs with his drink. He put his feet up on a matching ottoman and stared out at the frozen landscape, waiting.

Bjorkman, Traboldt, and Mason were all no-shows in the dining room. The occupants of the two in-use rooms were a 60-something man with a 20-something blond, obviously not his wife, and a couple who were here for ice fishing.

Later, as he pushed his plate aside and wished he could open a waist-line button on his pants, Connor had to give the chef credit. His braised venison with wild mushrooms and caramelized carrots was pretty damn good. Not $125,000-worth, but as good as anything one of his CEO bodyguard clients ever ordered from a multi-Michelin-starred restaurant.

But his trip wasn't wasted.

Two men had flown in after him with no bags, apparently here for the lunch as well. One was Emil Wissen, the manager of the Anchorage branch of Slossen Security. Connor had seen a picture of him that Judy had sent, and he was immediately recognizable — with his dark red hair and bushy, mountain-man beard.

In fact, maybe that explained why he'd flown here for lunch: to avoid recognition. The man he was with was older, maybe mid-50s. Rich and casual about it, but not effete. He was in good shape for his age — and it wasn't health-club good shape. He moved as if he could use his muscles if necessary. As if he were once a military operator.

Wissen was deferential to him, the way he'd treat an important client. Connor memorized the man's face and build so he could get someone to make a sketch of it later.

Both men had glanced over at Connor during lunch. To allay their suspicions, Connor had latched onto the only other lunch guest, one of the club's hunting guides. Connor played up his new-to-Alaska hunter status and pressed Johnny Garrison for the most interesting trips to take first.

Garrison looked like a young man an Alaskan father wouldn't mind dating his daughter. Clean shaven and boyish, but physically strong and confident.

Connor liked him, despite him recommending a bear and a moose hunt, not coincidently the two most expensive excursions. But he decided to give Johnny the benefit of the doubt. Maybe he really thought those would be most interesting to Connor instead of just most profitable for himself?

After lunch, Johnny slipped him a sheet of "Recommended Hunting Gear" and warned him that most "arctic" hunting clothes weren't protective enough for Alaskan weather.

Wissen and his guest left right after lunch in their private plane. Connor took his plane back a few minutes later. He waited until he'd deplaned in Anchorage to text Judy and ask for a good police-sketch artist.

An hour later, Connor opened his hotel room door to a middle-aged woman with goth makeup, big hoop earrings and a big wad of gum in her mouth.

Forty-five minutes later, he had a great sketch of the mysterious client.

Fifteen minutes after texting it to Judy, she called him back with a name. Jeremy Naylor was the CEO of a different security company.

"What kind?" he asked. "I hope to hell they weren't meeting about some secret merger that has nothing to do with Bjorkman or Mason."

"Hold your horses, hon," she said. "He runs the Bangnor Group, which you might have heard of. They're mercenaries. They do some small jobs themselves, but they also provide men to bigger companies like Triple Canopy, the Wagner Group, and Academi — which used to be Blackwater."

"What the hell?" Connor said, primarily to himself. He knew these groups from his Special Forces days. He'd fought beside some of their men.

"Exactly," said Judy. "Did we stumble onto something completely different, or..."

Connor interrupted, "...or are an Alaskan bar owner and Mason's ex-girlfriend somehow involved with mercenaries."

"If so, Mason really stepped his foot into a steaming pile of it. You want to brief Sara or should I?"

"I will. I'm going to tail Emil Wissen for a couple of nights, to see who else he's meeting away from the spotlight. I'll be sending you more photos soon.

"Meanwhile... just in case we have to get the inside dirt on this Bangnor Group, can you search it to see if Duke Gatlin is still working with them? He was there 13 years ago."

Connor hung up and sighed. He might need to call Gatlin, maybe even meet with him. He'd hated him back in Afghanistan, and he doubted the ensuing years had made the guy any less of an asshole.

CHAPTER TWELVE

Mason

It had been a day or two since he was put in this cell — he wasn't sure exactly.

Would Sara ever find him? Thus far he'd been transported on a boat, in a mini-submarine, and then in a van for at least four hours. He'd had a sack on his head, so he had no clue about the building they took him into. He only knew they'd marched him down three flights of stairs before dumping him here.

Then, other than throwing pre-packaged sandwiches and water bottles into his cell, they'd ignored him.

Well, it could have been worse. At least there was a functioning toilet in here. And the mattress didn't stink. Or leave bug bites on him. Although he would kill for a shower. He was starting to smell.

He had nothing: no phone, no computer, no old magazines to read, not even a Sudoku puzzle book.

Nothing to do but sit here and wonder WTF was going on.

He heard a key inserted in the lock and a bolt turn.

A giant of a man with a bald head came in, his gun pointed at Mason's face. He looked military, or former military, even though he wore civilian clothes. Were the two men who'd moved him from the boat mercenaries? There was something about the coordinated way they moved — as a team and as men who were used to using their bodies as weapons.

Mason stayed sitting on the mattress as ordered.

The next man through the door was surprisingly different. He was smaller, about 5' 8", skinny, with a mop of white-blond hair and an amused, condescending smirk.

"So..." he said. "I've been talking to your friend Emma."

Mason flinched. Was she in on this, or not?

"She tells me you're a brilliant hacker. That you're the reason your company, this 'Last Chance Investigations,' took down that sex trafficking ring some months back. That true?"

Mason just looked at him.

"I told her so-called brilliant hackers are a dime a dozen. I employ lots of them. But she said you could make them all look like amateurs."

Mason frowned. "Why would she be talking to you about my skills? I'm not looking for a job."

The man tilted his Albino-colored head of hair and his smirk widened. "She wanted to keep you alive."

Mason sat there, trying to understand his words.

The man grinned. "We only took you in case we needed to make her talk. It worked. She told us everything. Now, we don't need you anymore."

"Who the hell are you?"

He grinned. "Felix. Nice to meet 'cha." He moved forward and grabbed Mason's right hand and shook it.

The giant stepped forward, as if he could read Mason's desire to grab Felix and force him to tell where Emma was.

Mason stayed seated on the mattress and let Felix move his hand up and down in a parody of a hand shake.

Felix continued, "I run my own company, just like you. Mine specializes in data retrieval. We find and uncover things others want kept secret."

"Good for you."

Felix moved back and leaned against the door to the cell. "It could be good for you too. At least, it could keep you alive. If — and that's a big if — you're as good as Emma says you are."

"What about all those dozens of hackers you already have? They no good?"

"They're good. Thanks to them, we've got nine of the hot shots we need in the Alaskan State Legislature right where we want them. But there're three more, critical for our purposes, who still look squeaky clean."

Felix tossed his head and shrugged. "We can always plant something on them, if we need to, although that occasionally backfires. Since you fell into our laps, I figured we might as well give you a shot at those three. A chance to save your life."

Mason shook his head. "I won't work for you."

"No? Well, let's see." Felix pushed off the wall and nodded to the Hulk, who tossed a pair of handcuffs at Mason.

Felix said, "Put these on, then follow me."

Mason did so. Anything to get out of that cell. Felix led Mason out, with the giant holding tight to one of his arms.

Mason noted his cell and five other similar doors, all concrete block, covered by DRYLOC or something similar. His dad had used it on their basement walls to prevent moisture.

Felix started up a flight of stairs. Mason called up to him, "What did you want Emma to talk about?"

Felix stopped on the stairway and looked back at him. "She stuck her nose into something of ours, something she shouldn't have been able to find. Her idiot boyfriend told us that info was safe and that she was under control. Ha!"

He turned back and continued to the next floor. Since the walls on this floor were the same concrete, Mason assumed they were still under ground, although this floor appeared larger. Felix led them down a hall with five doors, and opened one of them, indicating Mason should enter.

The room was small. It looked like a small den with two comfortable chairs pointed at a huge, blank screen. The giant shoved him down into one of the chairs.

Mason knew that Felix had no intention of letting him live. He'd spoken far too freely for Mason to have any illusions abou that.

Felix leaned against the screen and grinned even wider. "Here's the thing you need to know," he told Mason. "We used you to get the answers we needed from Emma. And we got them. Now we don't need her anymore."

He was staring at Mason. "We'd planned to kill her."

Mason gasped.

Felix said, "We still will."

Felix screamed, his face scrunched up and going red. "She went to the fucking FBI!"

Then, like a switch that turned off, his anger disappeared. He moved to a small control panel beside the big screen and pushed a button. The screen cleared so Mason could see into the adjoining room.

Emma was there, her chest and legs tied to the chair she was in. Her head swiveled, looking around the room.

"Emma," Mason called, but she didn't hear him. Her eyes swept right past the screen, so she couldn't see him either. The glass must be one-way.

Two men walked into her room. Coming from behind, they each grabbed one of her arms. Another man in a lab coat came in and put a block of wood on the table in front of her. He squinted at Emma, then moved his index finger from left to right and back. He pursed his mouth.

Finally, he pointed at Emma's left side, and the man holding that arm brought it forward and laid her hand on the wood block.

Emma's eyes grew larger and her body jerked and twisted, trying to move her hand away.

The man in the lab coat pulled out a short-handled ax and slammed it down on Emma's left wrist, severing the hand, blood spraying everywhere.

Mason shot to his feet and ran towards the door. He had to get to her! The bald giant stepped in his way, and Mason swung his hand-cuffed wrists at the man's head — as hard as he could. But the man grabbed Mason's arms and squeezed.

Mason thrust a knee up, aiming for the guy's balls, but the giant twisted his body away. Instead, Mason kicked his shin.

The giant just winced.

Mason yelled louder than he ever had before and kicked at the big guy's knee.

Baldy let go of Mason with one hand and used it to punch the side of his thigh, stopping the kick and making him lose all feeling in that leg.

He brought his other leg up for a kick, and the giant punched him in the stomach — the pain of it paralyzing Mason. Then he let go of Mason's arm and shoved him to the floor.

Mason felt tears in his eyes as he convulsed, gasping to let in more air than the trickle that was coming through.

Emma! He put his hands on the wall and forced himself up, so he could see her. Her mouth was open, screaming, but Mason couldn't hear her. He looked at her wrist and saw someone had tied a tourniquet just above the bloody stump. The blood gush had slowed to a trickle.

He saw the man in the lab coat inject something into Emma's neck, and her body stopped jerking. The cords that had been clearly visible in her neck and arms relaxed, the muscles quieting. The other men untied her and lifted her still body up onto a medical bed that had been rolled into the room.

Mason turned his eyes to the skinny, little, blond man. Felix.

Mason had thought he understood hate — what it felt like. But he'd been wrong.

He stared at Felix. *You're dead*, he vowed to himself. *No matter how long, no matter the cost. You're a dead man.*

Felix smirked, undoubtedly reading Mason's mind. "You want to see her? Come on." He stepped past Mason and walked out the door with the giant, leaving it open.

Mason leaned against the wall, still gasping for breath and his right leg still numb. He hobbled along the wall and out of the room. Felix was standing by the door to the adjoining room, holding it open.

Mason rounded the corner and went into Emma's room, seeing blood everywhere. Her blood.

Terrified, he stumbled towards the bed and looked at her. He noticed her chest moving. She was breathing. He felt blood drain from his head and had to grab the bed to keep from falling.

He rested one hand on her red, sticky shoulder. Lightly. God forbid he woke her.

Shame washed through him — that he'd doubted her.

They'd threatened his life and she'd told them everything they wanted to know. She knew once she did, they'd have no reason to keep her alive. Or him. And so her last act was to talk up his hacking skills — so they wouldn't kill him. At least, not immediately.

He leaned down and rested his head against hers, gently. His hand on her shoulder felt essential, as if it would keep her alive.

"Here's how it's going to work," said Felix.

"We're moving you to a better cell — one with a shower." He scrunched his nose and added, "You need it. We're bringing you a computer and files with everything we already know about each of these three men."

"Emma?"

"As long as you cooperate, she'll get pain killers and antibiotics."

Mason turned and stared at Felix. "You didn't have to do this. You could have just threatened her."

Felix scoffed. "Of course I had to. I needed to know how you felt about her."

They stared at each other, then Felix shook his head and said, "I'm as far from stupid as you're ever going to meet. You think that I'd let you loose with a computer without knowing your attachment? And without you knowing in bloody detail just how far I'm willing to go?"

Felix pointed at the giant. "Joe Bob here and another man will be taking turns standing right in the room with Emma. Just so you don't get any ideas. At the first sign of trouble, they'll kill her. If the power goes out, or the phones, or there's any sort of commotion. Especially if they see anyone who shouldn't be here. Any sign of someone coming to rescue you, she's dead."

"But... this is Alaska. What if a storm takes out the power?"

"Then it's adios Emma. And you, too, of course."

Felix spoke into his phone, then another mercenary appeared. He and the giant looked so alike they could be brothers, except the new man still had hair.

"Take him to cell C and lock him in."

The new goon grabbed Mason's arm.

"I'll be down with the files and computer soon. You'll have six hours — then I want to see what you have."

Mason didn't acknowledge him. He kept his eyes on Emma until he was pulled out of the room and could no longer see her.

CHAPTER THIRTEEN

Sara

It was 3 AM when I arrived in Wasilla, a town just 50 minutes northeast of Anchorage.

Judy had called me earlier. Steve's software had captured a black Mercedes van on two traffic cams here, just an hour after our target van left Kitty's cafe.

Steve then hacked into the Wasilla airport camera and found the van entering the airport grounds, turning towards the private airplane hangers.

"And?" I asked her.

"And it's a small airport. No tower, just private planes, so they only had that one camera. It's close to Anchorage but without all the eyes on it."

"What makes you think this is it?" I asked.

"Well... the timing is right. And I betcha can't guess who owns one of the hangers."

"Judy...."

"Okay, okay. It's Schlossen Security. Funny how they keep popping up, isn't it?

"Did the van leave?"

"Two of them left the next day. One came back."

"How many planes have departed from here since then?"

"A bunch. And four helicopters. Maybe you can get a look inside and see which ones we should be following?"

"And..." she said, "aren't you glad I ordered all your favorite surveillance equipment overnighted to us two days ago?"

"Yes, Judy," I had to admit. "You're the best. I don't know what I've done to deserve you."

"Neither do I. You're such a lucky woman."

I drove our newly-purchased Jeep Cherokee SUV to the Museum of Alaska Transportation and Industry, close to the airport. I pulled up next to two trucks who were parked there, apparently overnight.

You might be wondering why we buy vehicles when we're on a case, instead of renting them. It's because of the hidden electronics that rental companies keep adding to their vehicles. The last thing I want is some gadget reporting exactly where I am at any specific time.

My phone vibrated. It was Connor. He told me that Schlossen Security's Emil Wissen had dinner tonight with the President of Alaska's state senate, then went home and stayed there. Connor was leaving to go get some sleep himself.

I rubbed my eyes, exhausted. Sleep sounded like a good idea to me too.

I walked into eight-foot-high brush to the south. After 300 feet, I came into the open and crossed Beacon Street. At this hour there was no traffic.

I continued safely back in the brush, until I reached Aviation Avenue. Just across it was the back side of five aviation hangers. One looked barely large enough to hold a single, small airplane, while another was big enough to house five or six. The one belonging to Schlossen was on the end, a mid-sized building.

Their hanger was covered in vertical aluminum siding, with no name or designation showing except the number "10." There were two windows on opposite sides of the hanger, the sills of each being about 14 feet above the ground.

I pulled out my infrared-detection glasses from the goodie bag Judy had prepared for me, and sure enough, the plain front door was covered by a camera, as was the small door on the northeast side.

There were no cameras on the southwest side of the building, which featured one of the high windows. The vertical siding left nothing to grab onto, in order to climb up. I figured the window was wired, but most likely set to warn only if it was broken — not if someone's face suddenly appeared next to it, looking in.

I could probably make it.

Wolves in the wild can jump up to 12 feet vertically, but the human record for women is just below seven feet. Fortunately, I didn't need to haul my entire body up 14 feet, I just needed to reach my hands that high and grab onto the window ledge.

I snugged the head harness for my PVS-14 night vision monocular tight on my head, and reminded myself I had an extra four plus inches sticking out the front of my face. I didn't want to slam my face into the wall and shove it deep into my eye socket.

There was plenty of room and paved ground, so I gave myself 15 feet and started at a slant towards the wall.

Full strength. You don't want to try this a second time.

As I drew near the wall, I thought of Mason, bent my knees, sprang up, and reached for that window as if his life depended on it.

Ow! Ow! Damnit!

My right fingers didn't make it, but my left fingers grasped a tiny inch of ledge. My face slammed into the wall — the monocular doing exactly what I'd feared, digging into my left eye. The head harness was askew, and I was lucky it was still on my head.

My fingers started to slip. Quickly, my hand turned into a paw with claws. Unfortunately wolf claws aren't pin-needle sharp like feline claws, but I dug mine in as hard as I could where the glass met the aluminum and they caught.

I used my right hand to adjust my head harness back into position, then turned it too into a paw and reached up, digging those claws into the ledge.

You should have done more pull-ups!

Shaking my head in disgust, I forced my arms to lift my body until I could see down into the hanger.

The glow from a nightlight by the side door and the light coming in from the two windows was more than enough for my monocular. A single one-engine plane was parked inside the hanger. One helicopter sat next to a spot big enough for another one.

I could also see two black vans with the rounded side profiles that Steve had said were Mercedes. And a muddy, beat-up-looking, boxy-topped van that must be a Ford. The latter would go unnoticed anywhere, but I bet the dented and dirty exterior hid an engine in excellent condition.

I stared at the plane and helicopter, trying to memorize their appearance, because I wouldn't recognize a brand name for either unless it was in neon lights.

I looked until I couldn't stand the pain in my claws for another second.

Should I break in and look for blood in the two vans? No. I didn't know enough yet to force a confrontation.

Where could they have taken Mason?

Back in my Jeep Cherokee, I drove onto Route 3 heading towards Anchorage. I passed a Wendy's, a McDonald's, a Sonic, the Brown Jug, and the Mug Shot Saloon, all closed.

"Mason would hate it here," I said out loud. It was 4 AM, the middle of the workday, for him. Weren't there any Alaskan night owls?

There were two pickups parked outside the closed Mug Shot Saloon. Maybe their owners had gotten lucky for the night? I pulled in beside them, then took out paper and tried to draw the features I'd spotted on the helicopter and the single-engine airplane.

The helicopter had a pointed nose instead of the rounded front I expected. It also had three side windows and what looked like a beanie cap on top with a rotor instead of a tassel.

I finished both extremely crude drawings, took pictures of them and sent them off to Steve and Judy.

I rubbed my eyes and yawned so big it hurt my jaw. Too bad nothing was open. A Diet Coke would help with the 45 minute drive back to Anchorage.

A flash of movement from the corner of my eye made me look up. A man — a very large man — was standing in front of my car with a Glock 19 pointed right at me.

CHAPTER FOURTEEN

Sara

The man with the Glock looked like the mythical giant lumberjack Paul Bunyan with a flannel shirt showing through his opened parka.

Another movement revealed a second huge man, standing outside my driver's window. This man's black face almost faded into the night, but his matching, suppressed Glock 19 in his left hand was crystal clear. His right elbow jutted out in a way that said "bullet-proof-vest-underneath" to me.

They both stood tall and looked at ease. Military. Or former military.

I looked at my dashboard. That's the problem with vehicles you buy over-the-counter instead of getting custom made. They don't come with armored steel and bullet-proof glass.

I could hit the gas and duck down — bullet-proof vests don't protect against an SUV running over you. I could also go with them, although that assumes they want to take me alive. I might wind up wherever they took Mason.

But that was too risky. If they hurt me bad enough, my body might transform and then... well... my odds of ever finding Mason would shrink to close to zero. As would my chance of ever again seeing the light of day.

"Get out of the car," the lumberjack said. I could hear him clearly through the crappy-thin window glass.

I popped the car door and carefully stepped out, staying close. I opened my eyes as wide as I could and raised my hands as high as they could go, letting them shake just a little.

"Ah, man," said the black guy. "She thinks she can play us with that scared-little-girl act. She must think we're dumb."

Oh hell. It usually worked so well for me.

"Though, in her defense," the man said to his partner, "you do look kinda dumb."

The lumberjack said "Stuff it" to his buddy, then used his gun and motioned for me to move away from the car.

"Come on. Someone wants to talk to you."

I lowered my elbows until they were at my waist, hands still raised. I used my hip to close the car door, then leaned my body against it.

Their orders were to bring me in.

"We can talk right here."

The black guy had backed up about six feet from me. The lumberjack had moved around the front of the car and was about eight feet away. I could see him better now, see his buzz-cut hair and his display of confidence.

They had me in an "L," completely fenced in with the car at my back. They could each shoot me without risk to the other man.

"Not asking," said the lumberjack. He tipped his head towards a dirty Ford van across the lot. "Get in."

I didn't need military training to know getting into the van would be a very stupid move.

I said in a calm voice, "No."

There was dead silence while I waited to see which man would move first.

Adrenaline rushed through my body. My hands vibrated. Sounds faded as a touch of breeze kissed my face.

I thought about my Ruger LC9, holstered right behind my back. I'd practiced drawing it as fast as I could thousands of times. Or I could go for the Spyderco knife in my boot.

My god, I felt so alive.

"Well..." the black man drawled. "We have to bring you in alive. But no problem if your kneecaps are shattered."

He pointed his chin at the lumberjack, whose eyes moved to my knees. He started lowering his pistol.

The black guy stepped towards me, his right hand reaching for my shoulder, while his left held the gun steady.

I dropped into a squat, so he grabbed at a shoulder that was no longer there, and I grabbed my Spyderco knife from my boot.

As the lumberjack lowered his Glock to aim at my knees, I launched myself at him. In my wolf form I can leap 16 feet horizontally, but not so much in human form. Still, this eight-foot distance was no problem. Instead, I used my wolf-given leg strength to add serious height to my leap, avoiding the bullet he sent to where I had been.

I was glad he'd been aiming low for my knees. Otherwise he would have hit something as I jumped.

I grabbed his head to stop my leap and came to earth behind him, still holding his head, now with only my left hand. I used my right to bring the Spyderco to the front of his throat.

Remember —at least one of them needs to stay alive to answer questions.

Sharp pain!

While I'd been making my move, the lumberjack must have pulled a knife because it was now buried deep into my right side.

Knowing I could heal the wound didn't make the pain any less.

He jerked the knife out and turned, aiming for my neck.

I slit his throat before it could reach me. Blood sprayed forward as if he were spitting it out. Holding him up in front of me, I ran towards the remaining man.

His shock bought me one second and he wasted another two firing into his partner before realizing the dying man's bulletproof vest was absorbing all the shots.

The black guy was quick for someone so big. I shoved his partner's body at his left side, putting my momentum behind it. I wanted it to hit him and his gun hand.

He sidestepped so his friend's body missed his gun arm entirely. Instead, it crashed into his right side, which he was able to turn slightly and thus remain on his feet.

I grabbed for his gun arm with both my hands, getting his wrist with one hand and the gun barrel with another.

It stopped my forward momentum, leaving me face-to-face with the man. I had a death grip on his gun.

Then it was a fight for control.

He was strong. More so than anyone I'd fought before. Maybe stronger than me.

A chill flashed through me.

Idiot! Since my transformation, I'd gotten used to being stronger than any man I'd fought. But they were all just ordinary men — not the military's elite. I'd never tested myself full strength against Connor, because he would have seen my strength as unnatural and I would've had to tell him my secret.

No time for regrets!

The man was winning. The gun was slowly turning closer and closer to where he could fire and hurt me.

I couldn't stop him.

I wasn't the big, tough woman I thought I was these past three years. I was physically inferior. Weaker. At his non-existent mercy. I couldn't even transform to wolf as I'd be helpless for a minute — plenty of time for him to kill or capture me.

The shock paralyzed me.

Wake up! Use your legs, dummy!

I focused my strength into kicking his left kneecap. There was a satisfying pop and crack, a scream, and a gunshot as his fingers squeezed the trigger.

I held even tighter onto his gun hand.

He started to fall, moved his left leg to stop it, then screamed again as he put weight on the shattered knee and crashed to the ground.

I landed on top of him, still holding the gun.

His fingers loosened and I pulled it from his grasp then knocked him on the head with the butt of it.

And again.

I pushed off him and stood with the gun.

Who knew how long he'd be unconscious? I didn't have time to search for all the other weapons he was bound to have. Even in Alaska, gun shots might cause someone to call the police. I needed to get out of here.

I got in the truck and pulled it around so my passenger side was as close to him as possible.

I jumped out with my phone and took pictures of his face and the dead lumberjack's. Then I grabbed the unconscious guy and struggled to haul him up and into the seat.

He was heavy, but I could handle that. The problem was his limbs. I'd heaved the top of his body up onto the seat, shoved his legs up into the air, and tried to squeeze the door closed. One of his legs flopped down, blocking the door.

Again I tried and again his legs flopped.

I wanted to slam the door on him. Finally, I pulled out my trusty zip ties — never leave home without them! — and bound his ankles together. I shoved them under the glove compartment where they stuck long enough for me to close the door.

Running around, I jumped into the truck and drove maybe a quarter mile, until I found a closed gas station. I pulled around the back and quickly fastened zip ties around his wrists. Then I used another to attach his wrists to the bar under the seat.

I sat back, catching my breath. I sent pictures of the two men to Judy, Steve and Connor.

Then I searched my prisoner.

The man was a walking armory. In addition to the gun I'd fought him for, he had two knives in his vest plus two guns on his ankles. His right one sported a holster similar to mine, inside his boot, while his left leg had a holster that wrapped the outside.

Interesting. I'd have to check that out for myself.

I pawed through his pockets and found a keychain and an I.D. card with his picture on it. My stomach dropped when I looked at it.

Oh crap. This was bad.

He didn't move a muscle or even an eyelid when he became conscious. The only sign was his breathing stopped for a second and his body froze. While before there were tiny, unconscious movements, now there were none. It was an easy tell.

"It's about time you woke up," I said. "I took six weapons off of you. Did I miss any?"

No answer.

"I especially liked your boot wrap holster. I might have to get myself one of those... and the brass knuckles you use as a keychain. I thought they were illegal everywhere, although, this *is* Alaska."

His eyes opened. "It's a keychain."

"Sure it is. Now, who hired you?" Mentally I crossed my fingers.

He stared at me.

I pulled out my phone and found a recent photo of Mason. "Have you seen this man? Maybe while you were kidnapping him?"

No response.

"If you tell me where he is, I'll let you go."

He shook his head. "You're in so far over your head."

"People keep telling me that. But I'm still here and they aren't. Do *you* want to be still here?"

He pulled his zip-tied feet up and kicked hard at the bottom right corner of the passenger window, shattering it. His boots scraped the remaining glass from the window edges.

I frowned. It didn't make any sense since the zip tie binding his hands was separately tied to the bar below his seat. All he'd do was make us both cold.

Then his hands came up, dangling the cut tie that had been secured to the bar.

What the hell?

He swung his bound hands towards my head, as if they were a baseball bat. I ducked and they glanced off the top.

I saw stars.

I grabbed his head and slammed it into my steering wheel, then into the dash.

He twisted, pushed up with his legs, and dove head-first out the side truck window he'd smashed open.

I stuck my face out of it to see.

He hit the ground, rolling sideways, taking most of the impact on his right shoulder. He jumped up on his feet, then dove behind the truck where I couldn't see him.

I closed my gaping jaw, pulled my Ruger and exited the truck. By the time I saw behind it, he was gone, his footsteps visible in the dusting of snow. The two zip ties that had bound his wrists and ankles lay there. Mocking me.

I picked them up and returned to the truck. In the light, I could see a jag in the cut that severed the plastic. It had to be a razor that went through half of it in the first swipe and the rest in the second.

Holy crap!

He'd had one, maybe two, razors hidden on him. I hadn't felt anything when I searched him. I'd never known anyone to hide razors before, so I'd never thought to look.

I drove 15 minutes south until I hit the intersection with South Glenn Highway, then took that road north, turning into the first place I saw, a closed coffee shop. I parked around back, out of sight, then did what I always do when I'm totally screwed and lost.

I called Judy.

"I doubt even you can help me this time," I told her. "My SUV has a kicked-out passenger window and some blood in the front seat that isn't mine."

My side twinged where I'd been stabbed, and ached as it started to heal. "There's probably some of my blood in here too. More important — the guy who kicked out the window is on the run just south of Wasilla. His partner, who tried to kidnap me, is lying dead outside the Mug Shot Saloon there.

"And... it gets better. I'm looking at ID for the guy that's still alive and it says he's a military contractor. Which means I could have a bunch of Army personnel after me any second now."

"Are you in the open?"

"I'm behind the Alaska Artisan Coffee Shop on S. Glenn Highway, right after it separates from the Parks Highway."

"I'll have someone pick you up in an hour. They'll come in a truck that you can drive the SUV into. You can ride with them back to Anchorage."

"Really? You can do that? Wait! Who will be driving and why can we trust them?"

"It'll be me."

Then she hung up on me, leaving me staring at my phone, my mouth hanging open.

How did she keep astonishing me? How did she always know what I'd need before I had a clue? And why wasn't she in Pennsylvania?

Oh... and thank god she wasn't!

Hiring her was the smartest thing I've ever done. I can't believe that I was so dead set against it.

Mason was right about her.

I swallowed. I just hoped I could tell him that someday.

CHAPTER FIFTEEN

Sara

I awoke to a soft knocking. I fumbled around and saw I was on bed sheets. Light through window blinds showed me I was in my hotel room at the Captain Cook in Anchorage.

I heard a click as my door unlocked. My LC9, which slept with me under my pillow, was already in my hand, so I slipped over the edge of the bed, putting it between me and the door.

Judy walked in and sat down in a chair.

I stood up and walked to the door. "I can't believe I didn't throw the safety bar on this last night."

"Sleep well?" she asked. "'Cause last night you looked like dog poop under my shoe. You fell asleep the second you sat in my truck."

"Cute." I rolled my eyes. "If you're going to wake me up, at least you could bring breakfast."

"Breakfast? Don't you mean lunch?"

My eyes widened and I looked at the nightstand. The clock read 11:30 AM. I couldn't believe it.

I sat down in a chair myself and rubbed my eyes. "Okay, I give up. How did you get a rental truck to me at three in the morning?"

"Girl, you can have anything you want in life at any time — as long as you pay some people to be on standby, just in case."

"And you paid a truck rental company owner "just in case"? How many others?"

"Read my expense report when I file it. And... are you really going to *complain* when I just saved your rear end?"

"No. No. It's just... a truck rental company?"

"Oh, puh-leeze. You needing new wheels in the middle of the night is almost a sure bet."

I stared at her, wanting to argue. But... she was right. I tried to hold back a grin, but the next thing I knew, I was laughing.

Judy joined in.

My stomach growled, complaining that it needed breakfast — no matter what time it was.

Then my eyes darted back to where she was sitting. Just looking at me.

"What's wrong?" I asked. "Why are you here?"

"Check your phone. We have a text from Mason."

"What?" I grabbed my phone and checked.

> My phone's blowing up with messages from all of you. Emma & I are taking some alone time, and we're turning off the phones. We're good. Give us some space. Geez!

I stared at my phone. *Could he? Really?*

"Oh hell no," I said.

"So you don't believe him either?" Judy sounded relieved.

"Did you talk to his mom?"

"She got the same message."

"Call Steve," I said, "and put him on."

Judy grabbed my laptop, opened it and stuck it in front of me. I leaned into the camera for a cornea scan and put my index finger on the secondary scanner.

Judy picked up my room phone and hit some numbers on it, then handed it to me. "Order yourself some food."

While I was doing that she sat the computer on the table and called Steve on it.

"Mason's text?" I asked when he came on the screen.

"He would never talk to his mom this way," Steve said. "He always asked her about her day, how things were going for her. Even when he wanted more space, he never would have said it like this."

I wanted to kick myself. "We never set up a code to use in case any of us were under duress. Why didn't we? We should have planned for this."

"Steve, did this really come from his phone?"

"Yes."

"But that doesn't mean he's alive, does it? Someone else might have sent it."

"I know how to find out," said Judy. She pulled out her phone and texted. "I just texted him to prove this was really from him by telling me the name of my cat. She misses him."

We waited.

A minute later all our phones dinged. It said:

> I'm sure Lola is happy with both you and Sara to pet her. Now I'm turning my phone OFF.

"It's him," Judy said. "And we know he's under duress."

"How?" asked Steve.

"Lola hates Sara."

Well, that was true.

"Steve," I said, "anything you can find about the location of that phone..."

"I'm working on it, but it isn't looking good. Meanwhile, you need to know about this Jabar Williams, the guy who escaped you last night. He and his now-dead partner work for ProCore Solutions, an I.T. consulting group that works primarily for the military.

"And, Sara, they're owned by Martes Empresas. I'm sorry. I should have been able to uncover them before. I didn't think to look at..."

"Steve," I interrupted. "Nobody cares about blame here. You found them. That's what matters. Although, now I'm confused. Martes owns a security service and a mercenary group — those make sense together.

Maybe even the Reindeer Bar. But a computer I.T. company? Although — they primarily work for the military, hmm....

"Okay," I said. "Assignments. Steve, in addition to tracking Mason's phone, find out what base Jabar and his buddy needed those passes to get onto. What's the connection between their ProCore Solutions and that base? And, while you're at it, why does a computer consulting company need two mercenaries?"

I looked at Judy. "Work with Steve to figure out who the head of Martes could be. I'm thinking he has to be former military — he's using his connections to support his companies. If you run into any dead ends, see if you can hack into the travel records for the CEOs of these three companies — Schlossen, Bangnor, and ProCore. See if in the past year they were ever in the same location as the same time. Maybe throw in the head of that Joseph Lake Sportsman Club, too."

"And?" asked Judy.

"If so, find out where each one stayed and see if some retired military bigwig was also there."

There was a knock at my door. I picked up my gun and said, "Yes?"

On the other side I heard, "Sara Flores? This is Special Agent Liam Stephans with the FBI. My partner and I would like to talk to you."

From my laptop, I heard Steve say "Holy crap" just before I closed the program and shut the lid on him.

Softly, Judy said, "This just keeps getting better and better."

"Show me your I.D.s," I said, moving towards the door.

This was not getting better. Connor would have called this FUBAR.

When their I.D. checked out, I invited special agent Stephans and his partner Olivia Newsome in and introduced Judy to them.

"What can I do for the FBI?" I asked.

"We're trying to locate Mason Spencer. We understand he works with you. "

"He does."

"You and he are partners in this Last Chance Investigations agency?"

"We are."

"Would you know where we can find him?"

"Unfortunately, no. Why is the FBI looking for him?"

Agent Newsome pulled out a picture of Emma Trabolt, her blond hair gleaming and her smile so Midwest-wholesome that you expected to see a few freckles on her nose. If she had them, she'd concealed up.

"Do you know this woman?"

"I don't know her and I've never met her. But she looks like a picture I've seen of Emma Trabolt, a girl who went to college with Mason."

"And you recognize her how?"

"Because Mason disappeared five days ago after coming up here to see her."

"And?"

"And I came up to Anchorage to ask if she knew where Mason was. But she appears to have disappeared herself."

Room service came to the door and I grabbed my breakfast. "Excuse me, but I'm starving," I said to the agents, stuffing a big forkful of scrambled eggs and sausage in my mouth.

Ah, protein!

Nobody talked as I chewed and swallowed. "So you're looking for Emma? Have you talked to her boyfriend?"

"I think you know he's disappeared as well."

I frowned and looked at my watch. It was April 19th. "His office said he'd be back at work today."

"Not anymore. They received a text saying he was taking the next two weeks off for vacation."

He waited but I said nothing.

Stephans asked, "Why haven't you filed a missing person on Mason?"

"Not my place. I assume that would be up to his parents."

"They said it was up to you."

"For all I know, Mason and Emma are off on some romantic tryst and her boyfriend is trying to track them down. Not something for the police. Or the FBI."

"But you don't believe that's the case, do you?"

"No." I stared at them. "Why are you here? Did someone file a missing person on Emma?"

The agents looked at each other and stood up.

Stephans took out a business card and handed it to me. "Please give us a call if you hear from either of them, or if you learn their whereabouts." They started towards my door.

To their backs, I asked, "Why is the FBI looking for Emma?"

They left without answering.

Judy's phone and mine rang simultaneously. It was Steve. "Can you talk?"

"They just left."

"I have a tap on the Joseph Lake Hunting Lodge. They just called the Talkeetna police. They've got Gerald Bjorkman's body. They said he hadn't returned to his room for two days. One of their trackers found him, frozen."

CHAPTER SIXTEEN

Judy

Judy promised herself she was going to kill Sara. Just as soon as she stopped freezing.

They'd flown here to the middle of nowhere Alaska in a claptrap plane that looked like it was made of paper. It had only one engine(!)

They'd landed on what was supposed to be a road underneath all the snow. It was amazing they didn't crash.

Judy nearly cried when the plane left them here, surrounded by miles and miles of snow and nothing else, except what looked like a tiny shack far off in the distance.

"That *shed* over there is your house? And I'm supposed to stay there?"

If this was how Sara planned to protect her, well... well, it was crazy!

"Where's the bellhop?" she whined, hugging Lola's travel cage close to her brand new pink snowsuit. She'd enjoyed buying all new clothes with Sara, until she saw she was going to look like a Michelin man — with a big puffy hat, big puffy boots, heck big puffy everything, including a big wrap around Lola's cage.

She'd tried to refuse the face mask but now, shivering in the cold, she was grateful Sara had insisted.

How could it be so sunny outside and this cold?

"You wouldn't need a bellhop," Sara said, "if you hadn't brought this huge suitcase."

As if, thought Judy. Sara had told her there were clothes in the cabin, but Judy suspected Sara's definition of "clothes" included stuff Judy wouldn't be caught dead in. Probably *sweatpants*, for heaven's sake. She shuddered.

Sara slung the strap for Judy's big suitcase over one of her shoulders and started off through the snow towards the shack.

How did she do that? Judy was only carrying Lola, and she didn't think she could make it. Sara was carrying Judy's luggage and a huge duffle-sized cloth bag of groceries.

She should have fought harder against this, but Sara had scared her. She'd said the case was heating up now with Bjorkman dead. She wasn't going to let Judy disappear too.

And....

Okay. Judy admitted to herself she had another reason for agreeing to come here. She had been curious about Sara's cabin — enough to want to see it.

She yelled at Sara's back, "How the heck did that old man come here? How would anyone find this place?" She yelled, even though she knew Sara couldn't hear her.

But Sara turned her head and yelled back, "Exactly my point. Nobody's going to find you here."

Judy was still a hundred yards away when Sara disappeared into the shack. She managed the remaining steps by saying, "Kill her, kill her, kill her," as she took each step.

A blast of welcome heat hit her when she entered.

"Oh, thank the heavens," she cooed, putting Lola down and starting to remove her mittens.

"Stay dressed for a little longer," Sara said. "I know it feels warm by comparison, but I keep it at 50 degrees when I'm away. I just turned up the thermostat."

"How do you heat this place?"

"I have two cold-weather heat pumps, one linked in as a backup, and a fuel oil heater in case the power goes out. I'll show you how to light that."

Judy looked around. It was much bigger inside than it seemed on the outside, thank goodness. It sure couldn't have been smaller!

Sara had tossed Judy's suitcase on the bed and started stowing all the food she'd bought. From the bottom of the huge bag, she brought out a cat litter box and a small bag of sand.

"Oh, thank heavens!" Judy set it up and let Lola out of the crate. The cat sniffed around and made an immediate deposit. Then she walked over towards Sara and hissed at her.

Sara turned and stared at the cat.

Lola hissed again, and Sara smiled.

"It's okay, Lola," Judy said, picking up the Persian and petting her. "That nasty woman is here, but don't you worry, Sweetie. She's going to leave so you won't have to put up with her much longer."

Sara finished stowing the food, then looked at her watch. "We've got about an hour before my ride gets here, so let me show you the cabin's defenses."

She moved to a wood-paneled wall about five feet from the door and pushed in. A two-by-three foot section of the wall opened up to display an electric panel with a screen. She flipped a switch and the display came to life, showing — no surprise — a snow-covered landscape.

"This camera is over the front door." She pushed buttons and three slightly different snow scenes appeared. "There's a camera facing in each direction."

Sara turned to look at her. "Don't worry about the cabin. It has steel walls that can stand up to pistols, rifles, and even an Uzi. Nobody can burn you out either. It looks like wood outside, but it's a plastic wood outer shell. That will melt, but under that is steel."

Sara stepped two feet closer to the front door and pushed a new section of wall. This one opened to reveal a six-inch deep cabinet that held two strange-looking rifles and several boxes of ammo. A dark screen at face level lit up when Sara pushed a button.

"This is a pin-hole camera, so you can see what you're shooting at."

Sara pushed another button and a metal iris opened. "This is where the rifle barrel goes. You can move it enough to cover 12 feet in height and about 20 feet in width. You won't be able to use the rifle sights, because the hole is purposely as small as possible. You have to use the screen to see where your bullets go."

Sara nodded at the rifles. "You told me your daddy trained you on rifles, right?"

"He took me shooting from the time I was 10."

"Pick one of these up."

Judy did, putting the stock against her right shoulder and inserting the barrel into the pin hole. She asked, "Why is the stock so long and the barrel so short? It's not even a third of the total length."

Sara smiled. "This is an FN PS90. The barrel is actually almost two thirds of the length. What you see exposed here is only a fraction of it."

She pointed and said, "Look here. It's an unusual safety. You're right-handed, so to engage the safety, you push this rotary dial forward. To fire, you pull the dial back towards the rear of the firearm."

She tapped a see-through piece on top of the gun that showed a row of bullets. "This is the magazine, which holds 30 cartridges." She pointed to an ammo box and said, "there are three more ready to go inside here."

Judy shook her head. "I don't know, Sara, this doesn't seem very well protected. What if bad guys are at the sides or back of the cabin?" She cocked an eyebrow at Sara, but couldn't hold back a grin.

Sara stared at her. "In that case, you'll want the grenades."

"Grenades? I was joking."

"I'm not." She moved back to the first, multi-camera panel and showed Judy four switches labeled "front," "back," "kitchen side" and "bed side."

"You've got three grenades you can launch in each of the four directions. One button press equals one grenade armed and launched. They are set to land 20 feet from the cabin so you don't damage it, only any attackers."

Judy smiled and shook her head. "How in the world did you get all this..."

"Connor had a friend who set it up for me."

Sara looked at her watch again. "Any questions? You should *not* need any of this, but just in case..."

Judy looked around. "Show me the secure Internet hookups and anything I need to know about the backup generator."

Sara showed her, then answered her phone. "My helicopter ride is almost here. I use this guy all the time, so my leaving should make anyone assume the cabin is empty. Just don't go outside. Someone could be watching, and you are way too vulnerable outside."

She added, "Just continue working with Steve and figure out where I need to go to find our Mason."

"You got it."

Judy watched Sara leave and secured the door behind her. She picked up Lola and sat on the bed, looking around.

"We'd better find them soon," she told the cat, "or I'm going to go stark raving mad in this place. I don't know how Sara stands it."

CHAPTER SEVENTEEN

Connor

Connor put his index finger inside his collar and pulled, trying to breathe a little easier. He hated bowties. Hell, he hated *any* neckties.

He knew it was psychological. He should have gotten used to them during his years as an executive bodyguard.

It's just that... whoever invented ties for men — bowties or the normal hanging-dick ties — had never worked in Special Forces. Once you'd choked a man to death, the idea of wearing your own garrote for someone else's convenience... well it was right up there with the stupidest inventions ever.

At least Juneau was south enough of Anchorage that he could walk around without ice and snow underfoot. He was not a fan of cold weather.

He glanced around the hotel ballroom, which was hosting the Governor's Charity Ball. There were colored lights, a soft-playing band, and women dressed in finery. The upper-crust men — tickets were $1,000 each — dressed with the most variation. He saw everything from office suits all the way up to tuxes.

Connor needed to know who else Emil Wissen was cultivating.

Influencing. A gala like this would give him the most leads in the least amount of time.

Connor kept at least 20 feet away from the man and made careful note of everyone Wissen spent any time with. After he moved on, Connor moseyed near the people he'd just left and used his lapel camera to get a face shot of each.

He nodded to the men and flirted mildly with the women, trying to leave as little impression as possible.

Three times he stopped as if his phone had buzzed him, then leaned back against a wall and sent the newest batch of photos to Judy and Steve.

One woman of an uncertain age, who'd worked very hard maintaining her looks, attached herself to him. Despite wearing a wedding ring set with a marble-sized diamond, she clinked wine glasses with him and started commenting on each of the people passing by. He'd tried to be polite and move on, but she put her left arm through his right and continued her monologue "chat" with him.

More extreme measures were needed.

Connor turned to face her and, making sure nobody else could hear him, smiled at her and said, "Darlin', I love that necklace. It goes so well with your dress, it's like it was made for it. Let me see your shoes."

Her eyes widened, her chatter stopped and her mouth opened slightly.

"Your shoes?" he asked again.

She pulled back the long gown.

"Perfect," he cooed. "Who's your stylist?"

Her lips looked like she'd tasted something bitter and she forced a smile. "So nice to chat with you," she said, then turned and walked away.

He controlled his face so there wasn't the hint of a smile, and continued trailing Wissen. This was the second time he'd used this tactic, and thus far it was a sure winner.

Not, he laughed to himself, that he'd ever recommend it — or even discuss it — with his old Army buddies.

An hour later, he saw Wissen get his coat and walk out the door.

He followed, in case the man met anyone else out here. But no, the valet brought his car and Wissen drove away.

Connor leaned against the side of the building and sent the last batch of photos.

He texted,

Any results yet?

Judy responded:

> I've attached names & titles to the ones we already know, in case you want to talk to them now.

He flipped through the photos she identified. He saw a U.S. senator, some state senators and several members of the Alaskan state assembly.

It was curious. Wissen had mostly ignored the business leaders in town who weren't also in a government post.

Well... back to work.

Connor returned to the gala and spent the next hour introducing himself to Wissen's contacts. He explained that he was new to Alaska, ran a boutique I.T. consulting company, and was considering hiring a security company. He confided that someone took a shot at him in Tulsa, where he was previously based.

Connor told each man he'd noticed him talking to Emil Wissen of Schlossen Security and wondered if they would recommend the company.

Each of them had responded, "Absolutely. His Schlossen is the top security company in the state."

However... there was a little hesitation — from each man. A pause right before they put on their politician smile and endorsed the guy. A pause that implied, "Oh hell no."

Later he told Sara, "I learned that each of them hated their dealings with Wissen and that each of them felt compelled to say good things about him.

"You're right," she said. "Wissen has something on them. Something strong enough that they have to do what he says."

CHAPTER EIGHTEEN

Sara

Steve and Judy called me early the next morning, at my Anchorage hotel room, the Captain Cook. I'd been half asleep, so I rubbed my eyes and pulled open the drapes. It was only 6:30 AM, but the sun had been up for a couple of hours. Right now it glared off the ice in the Cook Inlet, just a couple of blocks from the hotel.

"Tell me you've got a lead," I said.

"Maybe," said Steve. "The day after Mason disappeared, six airplanes left Wasilla that could be the one you saw in the hanger. It looks like they were all business flights. We might have to come back to them, but as for now, it's unlikely Mason was on any of them.

"The helicopter is a different story. It's an Agusta Grand, and only one of them departed Wasilla early that day. We've tracked down over 200 cameras in Anchorage, but none of them captured it.

"So we got creative. It would be too long a flight to anywhere if it went east. It could have been going north to Fairbanks, but cameras along the way in Talkeetna and Denali would have captured it, so we looked southeast. We found a webcam run by the Northwest Clean Air Agency that is focused on Mount Marcus Baker. A helicopter with the right shape flew past it at the right time. The resolution isn't clear enough to be 100% sure, but it never showed up in Valdez, so..."

I interrupted, "Steve, please don't tell me the how or why — just the result!"

"The result is the helicopter disappeared."

"What? You called to tell me you lost it?"

"There are only two options. If it landed at a private home, we'll never find it. But... Judy had another idea. You want to tell her?"

Judy chimed in. "If I was carrying someone I'd abducted, would I want to land at a house where I could be tracked and found? Heck no. But there's a ton of water out there. Maybe, I could land on a boat and just float away. Much harder to find me.

"So I wondered how big a boat needed to be to land a helicopter on it. It could be a small boat, but then the helicopter would remain sitting on top of it where it'd be easy to spot. I wanted a boat big enough to hide the helicopter after it lands. Because you were at their Wasilla hanger three days later, and it still wasn't back.

"So Steve checked out boat ownership for every potential player we've run into thus far — the hunting lodge, the restaurant, both security companies and the I.T. company those military guys work at."

"And?" I asked.

"Only Schlossen Security has a boat that qualifies and is cold-water adapted for Alaskan waters. Schlossen owns a 254-foot Legend expedition yacht, named the Intrepid, that has a helicopter landing pad that sinks down and gets covered completely with a roof. It's got two separate boat launch pads, and you can customize one of them to handle mini-submarines."

I considered it. "There's a lot of "ifs" in your thinking. But... the connection to Schlossen... we have to check it out. Where is the Intrepid right now?"

"It was last seen in Valdez Harbor, two weeks ago. Mason disappeared six days ago."

It felt like a punch to the gut, hearing "six days" out loud. A lot could happen to someone in six days. I sat there in silence. Steve and Judy were equally quiet.

There was a knock on my hotel room door. "Just a second. This should be room service delivering my breakfast."

I grabbed my gun, opened the door to the extent of the chain and looked through the keyhole at the same time. I hated looking through keyholes. I was sure someone would shoot me in the eye through one someday. But it was just a waiter.

I unlocked the chain and backed away.

The delicious aroma of sausages and eggs, not to mention the yeasty smell of the blueberry muffin all made my mouth water. I rushed the waiter out of the room and stared longingly at the food. Then I picked up the phone again.

"I'm back."

"Sweetie," Judy said, "do you want some alone time with your food? Should we call you back?"

That sounded wonderful to me, but...

"Funny," I said. "So if Mason was on that boat, what are the options for where he is now?"

Then I snuck a big bite of food into my mouth — a whole link sausage and a nice dash of egg with it. I closed my eyes in happiness.

Steve said, "He could still be there. In which case we'd need to find someone who could tell us yes or no. Or he could have been flown off later on the same helicopter — although, that's unlikely. If you wanted him somewhere else, the helicopter could have taken him there directly."

I grabbed another big bite of food.

Judy said, "He could have been taken off the Intrepid by a small boat. In that case, he could have landed anywhere within a small radius of the Intrepid that allows small boat landings. Or... if they do have a submarine dock and they took him off in that... He'd have a similar radius where he could be, but only where the coastline allows a deep-water docking."

I swallowed half a glass of O.J. while thinking.

"Okay," I said. "Steve, we need to hack their payroll to find employees who work on Schlossen's yacht. Look for someone who was on the boat when we think Mason was there, and who is off right now.

"Don't boats have to give their crew time off, like five months on and one off? Or at least a bunch of vacation days? Find me someone and I'll talk to them. They can tell us where exactly the boat was during the time period — or confirm it if you can find out some other way.

"We also need to know if there's a submarine dock on this boat, because that will affect where we search. And, if we're really lucky, we need to know whether or not Mason — or anyone — could have been there against his will."

Judy asked, "What do you mean?"

"Either because they saw Mason or because they know there were rooms that were locked and not to be opened by the crew."

I finished the O.J. "Judy, once we find out where the boat was within two days of Mason's disappearance, we'll need to search the coastline all around that area. Maybe deepwater. Maybe just a beach where a small boat could pull up."

Steve said "on it" and hung up.

Judy said, "You find me the area and I'll check the coastline."

Quick, before she could hang up, I asked, "Are we getting anywhere on the Bangnor Group, the mercenaries?"

"Steve and I are not finding any red flags on the company or on their CEO, Jeremy Naylor. Certainly nothing that would explain their part in this. Maybe they're not involved?"

"Somebody else has to be. I know Schlossen is bribing and threatening people and I think they decided to get rid of Emma because of what she uncovered at the bar. But I don't believe their CEO, Emil Wissen, knew anything about Mason disappearing. I should have been able to smell... uh *tell*... if he was involved.

"Somebody other than Wissen has to be holding him. A mercenary group like Bangnor would be exactly the people to handle it."

I sighed and added, "Talk to Connor. Ask him if it's worth him getting together with that guy he knew from Afghanistan — Duke somebody, wasn't it? I know he hates the guy, but maybe he should use that ridiculously-priced club he joined and take Duke hunting for a day or two. See if he thinks there's anything about Bangnor that can help us find Mason."

"I'll do it right now."

"Wait a second, Judy. You doing okay at the cabin?"

"So far," she replied. "But if I'm stuck here much longer, I'll start seeing things. You got any abominable snowmen out here?"

I grinned. "Not to my knowledge. But if you run into one, you might run instead of flirting with him."

"If he's male, he can be flirted with."

She hung up on me.

CHAPTER NINETEEN

Sara

It took me six hours to drive from Anchorage to Valdez, the town where the crew of Schlossen's Intrepid maintained a two-bedroom apartment. It was 5 P.M. when I arrived.

By looking at older job postings, Judy had found the Intrepid had a 4/1 policy, which means the boat crew would serve four months on the boat then have one month off. She'd gone on various job boards and found boats of this size who offered a 4/1 or 5/1 crew policy typically had a rental apartment in their home city. The apartment could be used as a convenient spot for supplies to be delivered, or for a day or two by the crew going on their one month vacation or coming back from it.

Intrepid had such a rental apartment in Valdez.

Judy said Valdez temperatures were reaching 42 degrees during the day right now. But nobody with a full month off was going to hang around a 3,800-resident town for longer than it took to wait for the next plane or boat out.

"Fun fact," she texted me. "In the last 12 years, the population has shrunk by 111 people."

I grinned. Valdez was not on Judy's "to visit" list.

Steve found 26 crew members on their payroll, excluding the captain. Two of those crew — an ETO boat electronics guy and a stewardess — started leave yesterday. He sent me pictures of both of them.

He also checked each of their finances and found they were both dirt poor. The stewardess had $2,000 total in her bank accounts, while the electronics guy, who made $100,000, was paying alimony to two ex-wives and child support for three kids.

The stewardess, Bethany Willis, answered the door of the apartment. I told her that I was searching for the asshole who ran off with my little sister six months ago, and the family hasn't seen or heard from her since. I said I got a tip from someone who thought they saw him on the Intrepid last week.

"I'll give you this $500," I said, showing her five one-hundred-dollar bills, "just to have coffee with me right now. If you can help me find him, there's a lot more I can give you."

We ended up going through the drive-thru at Klondike Coffee, a small blue box of a building isolated in the middle of a parking lot big enough to handle multiple semi-trucks. The window where you placed an order was on one side and you drove a 180 around the box to get to the pickup window on the opposite side.

I laughed at a prominent sign that said, "Support your local caffeine dealers."

Drinks in hand, we drove past a parked oil tanker whose driver was shoveling what was probably the Jimmy Dean sandwich down his mouth. We parked at least 50 yards from him and sipped our drinks.

Their chai latte was pretty darn good. Bethany looked like she was enjoying her "Winter Solstice," which included white chocolate and blueberries.

I pulled out $10,000 in cash and showed it to her. "It's yours if you can help me. Where was the boat this past week — starting Monday?"

"I don't know exactly," she said, "but we stayed around here, going into some coves. We never left the Prince William Sound, but it's a pretty big Sound."

"The tip said they saw him five or six days ago on your boat — on Monday or Tuesday. Maybe Wednesday."

She asked, "What's he look like?"

For $10,000, I figured she might pretend she saw him, so I said, "Just describe all the male guests you had during those three days."

She did. They were light on guests that week, and she only saw four non-crew males over those dates. All middle-aged, paunchy, and puffed up with their own importance.

"They weren't rich-rich," she said. "Their clothes were high end but not exclusive. They looked like politicians to me."

I broke out half of the $10,000 and told her I'd give it to her regardless of whether or not she recognized the man from my photo. Then I showed her Mason.

She looked at him, then at the $5,000. I smiled and handed it to her.

"No, I didn't see him at all. I would have noticed him."

I said, "Suppose he didn't want to be noticed. Were any of the cabins off-limits to you?"

"Sure. Schlossen is a security company, so sometimes the rooms on B-Deck are off limits. They hang a sign at the entrance to that section and we don't clean those rooms or do turndown or anything, until the sign is removed. They use the rooms to protect clients who are in danger. Until the company can make it safe for them to go home."

I asked, "The sign was up this past week?"

"Just Monday and Tuesday."

"How would such a person get on or off the boat?"

"Guests arrive almost exclusively by helicopter."

"Did one arrive this week?"

Bethany looked at the remaining $5,000 in my hands.

I nodded. "It's yours if you answer this and a few more questions."

"It's been a few days since a helicopter landed. Three or four? Wait. It landed right when the sign went up for those B-deck cabins."

"When did it leave?"

She frowned. "I don't think it has. I don't remember hearing it."

"Did one of your small boats take off a day or two after the helicopter arrived?"

She pursed her mouth. "I don't think so... although if it left in the night and came right back, I wouldn't know."

I looked at her, hoping for more.

"Oh, you know what? The minisub left. I didn't see it back in its slip until two days ago."

Son of a gun.

I handed her the final $5,000 and drove her back.

We didn't have any other leads, so I decided to believe in this one. To believe they'd taken Mason someplace right on this Sound, someplace where it was deep enough for an underwater dock.

I pulled to the side of the road, stopped and took out my map. Prince William Sound was huge, with what looked like a hundred or more coves. Would there be maps of the area that show shoreline where the water was at least eight feet deep — probably more like 10 or 12 — right at the edge?

If not, we were screwed trying to follow this lead any further.

I suddenly felt light-headed. It'd been seven days since they took Mason and every single lead thus far had turned into a dead end. What if this one does too?

What more could I do? I put my head in my hands and squeezed my eyes to stop the tears.

How could I be this incompetent? Mason was depending on me.

CHAPTER TWENTY

Mason

Mason sat beside Emma's bed and gently held her right hand. They'd put a clean dressing on the stump, where her left hand should have been. Today no blood spotting was visible, but some kind of clear fluid was leaving wet spots.

He laid his head down on her arm and closed his eyes. They gave him an hour with her, twice a day, but he never knew if she would be awake or asleep. He needed her awake — he needed to know she was still there. Still herself. He craved talking to her as much as he needed air to breathe.

But...

Sometimes when she was awake, her pain broke through the drug she was being given. He couldn't stand to see that. And even if the meds were working....

It hurt to look into her eyes. He needed to rescue her — get her out of here and to a real doctor. But how?

He knew Sara and the team were looking for him. They would have seen through the text Felix had made him send, claiming he was on a vacation.

But how could they find him without him there to track down the clues?

It *killed* him to sit each day at a brand-new ThinkPad running Linux, with all the best hacking apps, and do nothing about his and Emma's situation.

Okay, not exactly nothing. He'd uncovered roughly where he was now — right in the middle of nowhere. Not that far, actually, from Sara's property in Alaska. Wasn't that ironic?

He could get the location to Sara — probably without being caught. They had a keystroke tracker for everything he did on the computer, but he was pretty sure he could get a message out and make it look innocent.

The problem was Felix and his goons. One of them was stationed right outside Emma's room at all times. His orders were to kill Emma if anything happened that indicated the site was under attack. If he heard gunshots... if the lights went out... if phones cut out.

Now, maybe, he wouldn't be quite that fast. Nobody would thank him if a storm cut out the power and he killed Emma. He might try to take one more step to evaluate whether or not they were actually under attack.

But Mason couldn't bet Emma's life on it.

He felt Emma's arm move. Her eyes opened and he was frozen by her pale, blue eyes that always reminded him of the anemone flowers his mother grew.

"Mason," she said, her eyes looking around the room. "The FBI..."

Mason moved closer to her face and squeezed her hand. He was sure the room was monitored visually and with audio. He shook his head from side to side with as little movement as possible. He stared in her eyes and said, "Don't worry. You already told our captors everything about your contact with the FBI. You just need to get better now."

Emma's eyes widened. She pulled her right hand free from Mason and scratched her left shoulder — staring at him and then looking at her hand. Mason saw she was scratching with only two fingers, the others folded down.

He tried to control his surprise. He was suddenly back in early computer science classes, where they learned Python, and used it to run a Caesar Cypher. The code was very simple and took it's name from Julius Caesar, who reportedly used it to send secret messages by courier. You needed to designate how many letters over to shift. Emma had just used two fingers — so the shift was two. That meant an "A" would be represented by a "C" which was two letters over.

She pulled him down to her and whispered in his ear, letter by letter. Mason shifted each letter back. Translated, she told him, "FBI file LHU hidey."

Mason gave the hint of a nod. The college where they'd met, Lock Haven University, had a server the computer science students used. He and Emma had hidden files in it for fun, competing to create the better hiding spot with the most innocuous names, that were least likely to be noticed or deleted. They'd called it their "hidey-hole." Emma must have hidden a copy of the financial files she uncovered there for safekeeping. And she hadn't told Felix about it when he interrogated her.

His eyes burned. Emma didn't think she was getting out of here. She was asking him to get those files to the authorities in case she didn't make it.

Out loud he said, "Yes, I'll tell your parents you love them, even your bratty kid brother. But you're going to tell them yourself. You just need to get stronger. Please rest."

She nodded and closed her eyes.

He looked at his watch and found he still had 15 minutes. He scooted closer to her bed so he could continue holding her hand. Then he stretched back in the chair and rotated his neck.

Fifteen minutes to figure out what to do about his current search.

They had him looking for dirt on two Alaskan senators and one committee chair that looked squeaky clean, even after Felix's people tried their best.

It took Mason two days, but he'd found real dirt on one of the men and it was bad enough that he was happy to turn it over to Felix. The senator, George Usher, had hidden it so well that Mason almost didn't find it. He must have a separate computer locked away that he only used for the dark web and a revolting child-sex-video site. Usher had slipped up just once — maybe he needed his "fix" —but that was enough for Mason to track his username on the site to a burner phone used within 50 feet of the guy's home.

It wasn't enough for law enforcement to arrest him, but armed with the username and pictures from the web site — he knew Felix's goons could control the man.

No, Usher wasn't the problem. Senator Winston was. Mason had grown impressed while researching the man. His record was the kind you'd want from a state senator, helping those in his district who most needed it. He was actually living on his $50,000/year salary, with a tiny little boost two years ago from a book he co-authored on protecting the environment.

But Mason had found a possible weakness. When he was just eleven, Winston's family had moved towns and joined a new Catholic Church. Soon afterward, Winston traveled south to Minneapolis, where he stayed for a year with his uncle's family. Knowing his keystrokes were being tracked, Mason slid over that and started digging into young Winston's time with his uncle.

Mason suspected the boy had been abused by a priest at the new church and that's why he was sent away. He could confirm it by investigating the priests at the church, but then Felix would know and he would use it against Winston. Who knew how traumatic that could be for the man? Mason didn't want to help them do that.

Joe Bob, the mountain-sized bald goon, came in and tapped Mason on the shoulder. His time with Emma was up.

Mason leaned over and kissed her forehead. He was pretty sure she was still awake but she'd kept her eyes closed.

He followed Joe Bob who led him, not towards Mason's cell but to Felix's office. Good. He'd tell Felix he'd hit a wall on Winston and there might not be anything to find. He'd recommend moving on to the third person now. He'd say he could always come back to Winston.

Mason didn't want to give them Winston, if what he suspected was true. The man deserved his privacy. But if it came down to Winston's secret or Emma's life — he was choosing Emma. Even though he knew he'd only be buying one or two more days for her. Felix was never letting her out of here. They'd kill her — and him too — as soon as they'd gotten everything they wanted.

The only question was whether Sara would come for him sooner than that. If so, they'd both die sooner. How could they launch a rescue that made no noise? It's why he hadn't risked contacting Sara. And yet...

He couldn't make himself tell Sara *not* to come.

He despised himself for waffling.

CHAPTER TWENTY-ONE

Sara

I'd texted Judy to find me every cove in Prince William Sound where it was at least eight feet deep right where the water reached the shore. I told her not to wake me for at least four hours, then grabbed a nondescript motel room and passed out.

It was dawn when I woke up. My phone was crammed with texts.

Connor told me he was on a day-hunting trip with the, quote, "asshole he'd worked with from Bangnor Group."

Judy had sent me five separate texts, spaced out over eight hours:

> Did you know there are 3,800 miles of shoreline in PW Sound? You owe me a raise! Plus — I just spent your big bucks to get a passel of NOAA nautical charts.

> There are 45 different locations on the Sound with deep water at the shoreline.

I narrowed it down to the two locations I just
emailed you — because there has to be a
building there for an underwater dock to make
sense.

I chartered you a boat and captain in Valdez
— it's yours for today and tomorrow. Details in
the email. I told him no crew so you'd have
fewer nosy people for the trip, but you can tell
him otherwise.

And... don't call me for six hours. I need my
beauty sleep.

Captain Pete Kakee was a wiry man of few words, his height no
greater than mine, but his body deceptively strong, like a lightweight
MMA fighter. I guessed his age to be around 50, but I could be way off.
He was at least part Native Alaskan, which would make him look
younger, but his face was aged by constant exposure to the weather.

I don't know much about boats. This one was named Fortuna and was
about twice as long as I can jump, given a running start, which made it
about 32 feet. It had that little house thing on top where you could steer
and remain hidden from the elements on all sides, except the back entry.

I showed him the two coves that I wanted to see, and we took off
for the first. I was bundled up for the trip, but the wind felt like icicles
scratching my cheeks. I went below and searched the cabin — just in
case anyone was hiding there.

Who, me? Paranoid?

Soon the rocking of the boat, the fumes, and my traitorous
stomach made me go back up on top before I embarrassed myself by
throwing up.

I held out my map in question to Pete. He pointed ahead to the
left, then pointed on the map to the Tatitlek Narrows. He steered us
into it.

Land closed in on each side and I startled at movement to my
right, where two moose were pawing at the snow. I showed them to
Pete.

"Moose are the squirrels of Alaska," he said.

Okaaay...? "Thanks for that philosophical wisdom."

We motored along for another 20 minutes before he pulled into the cove I'd requested.

"Just steer along the coastline," I said.

There was a foot or two of gravelly beach on one side of the cove, but as we motored around to the other side the beach disappeared, and a rock wall came up directly from the water.

There was one house there, atop the rock face — about 10 feet above the water. I pulled out my T-7 thermal binoculars and looked for heat signatures, but didn't find any.

I sighed. I'd hoped Mason would be sitting there, just waiting for me to rescue him.

Pete turned the boat away and out into the cove so we weren't so close.

I asked, "Why move away. Do you think the owner will shoot at us if we're too close?"

He raised an eyebrow at me. "Doubt anyone's home. The shutters are closed tight."

I cocked an eyebrow back at him. "Well, then?"

He looked at me, and I could see the questions he hadn't asked, about why I wanted to see these two specific sites.

I said, "I'm just curious how they get into the water."

He tilted his head letting me know he wasn't buying it, but he pulled the boat closer to the rock ridge the house sat on. I looked into the water and didn't see anything. I had no clue how a mini-sub dock would look, but the water here was clear enough that I'd have seen it. I think.

I said, "There aren't any roads out here, are there?"

He shook his head.

"So how do they get to the house? Pull back and let's see if they could land a plane behind."

We pulled back into the middle of the cove. There was land behind the house with no obvious trees or bushes.

"Think they could land a single-engine there?"

He said, "Only if that ground is smooth. Or they could use a helicopter."

I shrugged. "Okay, let's go see the second site."

Something sharp bit my face. I slapped at it and came away with a dead, fat, bloody bug on my glove.

Pete laughed. "This is Alaska, where even the mosquitos are bigger."

I rolled my eyes then went below for a paper towel to clean my glove. I hoped the next site would give us clearer answers.

Did we need to search with a drone? That made me remember a past operation when Mason had a drone waiting for me in the airplane I took to Arizona. And that caused my eyes to water, so I rubbed them and swore at Mason for leaving us like this.

I wondered if I could assign him a bodyguard for the rest of his life. Assuming we got him out of this.

I took a deep breath. We *would* get him out.

I came back up 40 minutes later, when the engine noise changed and we slowed. We were back closer to where we'd started, in Long Bay, which is two bays over from the one leading to Port Valdez.

Pete looked over as I came up to him.

He said, "Gotta question for you. That Judy Street gal who works for you. She married?"

I grinned. "Nope."

"How old is she?"

I raised my eyebrows.

He said, "I mean, she's not real young, is she? Not in her 20s?"

"Nope," I said, smiling even bigger. "She might like you. It's worth a try."

He nodded and pointed ahead. We passed an island right in the center of the bay. When the water forked, we took the left passage and, again, passed a centered island. Again we went left into yet another cove, with yet another island in the middle.

"What's with the islands in the center of each of these coves?" I asked.

"We put them here just for the tourists."

I looked at him. "So you don't know the answer either?"

He ignored my question. "You want me to circle the shoreline, like we did at the last place?"

"Please."

In this inlet, of an inlet, of an inlet, there were two buildings, the biggest being a boxy square, maybe 20 square feet, close to the edge of an eight-foot rock face. About 25 yards past it was a shed or boathouse big enough for two boats, with a launch ramp down into the water.

Although the main building looked commercial, there was no sign anywhere on it. The windows were closed tight. I looked for cameras but couldn't see any., which didn't mean they weren't there.

Again I used the thermal binoculars and, again, there were no heat signatures inside.

I couldn't see anything in the deep water in front of the main building.

This spot also had no roads, so we pulled back to get a better view of the land around the place. It was heavily forested, with just one small, clear patch. No airplane was landing here, no matter how small and nimble. Helicopter, boat, or — maybe — mini-sub were the only means of arrival or departure.

I turned to Pete. "It looks commercial to me. How about you?"

He nodded. "Someone could live there, but it's not primarily a house."

"Then wouldn't you expect to see a sign of some kind?"

"Maybe. Maybe not. We got a lot of people up here don't want anyone in their business."

I shook my head in annoyance, pulled out my phone and took some pictures. Then I told Pete to take me back to Valdez.

I moved to the end, or was it aft?, of the boat and used my sat phone to call Judy. I sent her the photos and asked for everything she and Steve could find on the two places, especially the owners.

Then I went below and hoped they'd find me a new lead.

Soon.

CHAPTER TWENTY-TWO

Connor

Going hunting with Duke (Asshole) Gatlin was a terrible idea. Connor wished for the hundredth time that he'd pushed back when Judy suggested it.

It sounded like a good plan. It was logical. They needed to know if -- and, if so, how —Bangnor might be involved in Mason's disappearance. Duke was one of their mercenaries, so Connor should be able to get an idea about the company from him.

It worried him that some part of the military was involved in Mason's kidnapping. That two military guys had tried to grab Sara. That the Bangnor Group could be involved.

But Duke made his skin crawl. He'd forgotten how bad it was dealing with the man. Or maybe it was worse now. The bluster. The pretend-joking barbs. The bone-deep need to believe he was tougher and better than Connor.

The instant Connor heard his voice on the phone — after 13 years — he knew he wanted nothing to do with the guy.

Yet, here he was.

The plane to Joseph Lake had been excruciating, all hearty hellos and pretend camaraderie. He'd discovered the only thing more disgusting than Duke being his normal asshole self, was Duke and he fake-smiling at each other.

He'd used the time to ask Duke about working for Bangnor, Connor pretending he might consider it for himself. He asked about the money, the jobs, and the guys. The money was pretty good. Not up to what Connor had made as an executive bodyguard, and certainly not what Sara paid.

He didn't ask what he most wanted to know — why Duke had agreed to spend a day with him. What was *his* goal for this meeting? Because it sure as hell wasn't catching up with an old friend.

At the lodge, they'd met up with the club guide, Johnny Garrison, who checked all their gear and weapons. Then they hopped a helicopter to this location 10 miles away. Johnny said it was a good spot to find a grizzly bear.

Connor had sized Duke up more carefully on the helicopter, as they'd soon be alone in the middle of nowhere each toting high speed rifles powerful enough to stop a grizzly. Worse, Johnny would be there with them, trapped in the middle of something he knew nothing about.

Duke had a few gray hairs showing on his buzz cut and in his trimmed beard. He was two inches shorter than Connor's 6' 4", which had always ticked the guy off. Connor would notice him standing as tall as he could, whenever they were near each other.

Duke had dark hair, dark eyes, and a dark disposition. And over-kill macho tats on his bulked-up arms. He'd gained a few extra pounds in his gut over the past 13 years, but it was obvious that he still worked out — hard.

They'd landed on a snow-packed clearing, surrounded by forests of lodgepole pine trees, their branches weighed down with ice. Connor nodded as he watched the helicopter fly away and leave the three of them. At least he could stop smiling at Duke. Maybe the guy would try something.

Hell, the bad guys wanted to kidnap Sara and they did get Mason. Maybe Duke would try to take him. Or just shoot him.

Let him try, thought Connor. *Please.*

CHAPTER TWENTY-THREE

Sara

I paced my hotel room in Valdez, stopping to look out the window. It was 6 PM, but the sun was still high in the sky.

It'd been five hours since I sent Steve pictures of the commercial building located about as deep into Long Bay as you could go on the water. The place where a small boat or possibly a mini-sub had delivered Mason.

I looked at my phone and wanted to call Steve, badly. But I'd done just that two hours ago, and he'd shut me down, saying he'd said he'd contact me the second he had anything. He couldn't keep wasting time taking calls from idiots.

Okay, he didn't use the word "idiot" but his meaning was crystal clear.

Should I stay here? Go back to Anchorage?

This was the most frustrating case I'd ever had. So many suspects. So many leads that thus far hadn't got us anywhere near Mason.

Schlossen was involved up to their necks, but it never led to Mason. Unless they owned one of these buildings?

Maybe Connor had found out something from the guy he hated so much who worked for Bangnor?

If I couldn't bug Steve, I decided to bug Connor and called.

"Hi," he said.

I heard a growing roar in the background. "What's the noise?"

"The chopper is picking us up."

"Did anybody shoot anybody?"

"Still time for that. Just a second."

A few seconds later, he came back on. "Sara, we've got to push this, because I feel like we're getting nowhere. I'm going to go drinking with him tonight. Maybe meet up with some of his team — pretend like I miss it and want to hear stories about what it's like today."

"Good idea — except you'll be alone and he won't."

"Yeah, but I'm me and he's an asshole."

"Cute. Talk to Steve..."

"Already did. I'll be loaded up with trackers."

I sighed. "Trackers won't do a damn bit of good if nobody is close to come to your aid. I'll shadow you. Follow the trackers."

"Don't screw the op by getting too close. They'll be looking."

I rolled my eyes. "Do you know how insulting that is — that I'd screw up your op?"

"About as insulting as you implying I need you for backup?"

The phone was silent as I regretted I couldn't put a fist through and land it on his chin.

"Everybody can use backup."

"You're right. Sorry. Duke has me spoiling for a fight."

"Okay," I said. "I'll coordinate with Steve and give you a wide perimeter backup. But one thing you should know."

"Yeah?"

"Protect yourself. If you let someone get the best of you and end up kidnapped like Mason... or dead... I will never let you hear the end of it."

I heard a chuckle. "Well, damn, guess I'd better bring my A-game."

He cut the connection.

I looked around for anything not already in my suitcase and threw it inside. I was just zipping it up when my phone rang again.

It was Steve.

Finally.

I sat down on the bed.

He said, "I'm pulling Judy in on this call. Sara, I think we've found him — the guy behind all this. Probably the silent owner of Martes Empresas and the guy owning the mercenary group, the bodyguard business and an I.T. group that contracts with the military."

I closed my eyes in relief.

"His name is Neville Huber. He has a little company that owns that building on the Sound you found, owns a ton of Alaskan land, and has connections with each of the other companies we've found."

"Did you find video of how they took Mason away? Because there's nobody there now."

"Sorry. There's no video anywhere near that building. No roads. No cameras. Nothing. Which is probably why it's there."

Judy butted in, "This Huber is richer and more powerful than the heads of Bangnor Group or Schlossen Security. So he's more likely to be the head honcho, not a peer. He also has the best military connections. His daddy owned 200 acres of worthless Texas land that — thanks to fracking — he now leases out to oil companies for a fortune."

"Send me the details, but for now all I want to know is where he might be holding Mason."

Steve said, "I'm into his financials and looking at everything he owns. But it's a lot. We already checked out the Bangnor and Schlossen holdings and didn't see anything remote enough for holding hostages. Now we're starting on buildings owned by the I.T. company."

I interrupted, "Start with anything he owns outside of those three, like this commercial building we just found. If nothing pops on that, then focus on the I.T. company. But, first, I'm going to shadow Connor, so I need to know where his trackers are in real time."

"I'll send you the app to download and you can track him from it. We've got three on him: one in his phone, one in his shoe and one on his body. But, Sara... you'd better hope they go to a big town like Anchorage. If he goes to a military base, you're not getting in. Also, if he goes to one of the small towns in the center of the state, like that hunting lodge is... well those towns have maybe 200 residents and they all know each other. You can't hide in a town like that, and it's a killing cold out there."

"Hiding is one of my super-powers. I need Judy to stay on the line, but you go and find where he's holding Mason."

I heard Steve click off, then nothing.

"Judy?"

"I'm here. All alone. Nobody to talk to but my cat. Nothing but snow to look at. Bored to the point of being comatose."

I rolled my eyes. "Drama queen."

"Seriously. Me and Lola are leaving this prison in 24 hours max. Safe or not."

"Then give me some of your miracle Internet searching. Look for any business, location, company — anything ever connected with this Huber guy. Hopefully Steve will turn up places he owns where someone could be stashed, but some might be off the books — in which case it'll be up to you to find him."

"Oh," I added, "also get me a helicopter on standby for the next 24 hours. Have him ready to pick me up here, as soon as the tracking tells me where Connor has gone."

"I'll call the guy I already have on standby," she said and hung up.

I smiled. Of course she already had a man on standby.

CHAPTER TWENTY-FOUR

Judy

Enough!

Judy had lasted two days — 48 *long* hours in Sara's cabin. Now what?

The first day, she spent hours trying to compile bits of info from Steve into a coordinated timeline for all the CEOs, what city each of them were in and when. She also started a search for the richest retired military officers, not men who just served in the military, but those who hit at least Captain. Preferably Colonel or General.

Last night she spent ten hours going blind, looking at water depth charts.

This morning she exercised, petted Lola to distraction, and because she hadn't heard from Sara, spent three more hours learning Hand Talk.

She was pretty much at her personal limit for being isolated. She'd even gone over all of Sara's paranoid security features again, and cooked a pretty good stew that she planned to reheat for lunch today.

She was just about to start screaming in boredom, when someone pounded on the door.

Oh, no!

Judy ran to the panel with the video and turned it on. There was nothing there. No, wait, was that... was there a... a single gray wolf right outside her door?

Judy looked at the other cameras, but she didn't see anything else.

But... who pounded on the door?

Movement from the first screen caught her eye. The wolf stood up on its hind legs and pounded both front paws on the door.

What the...? It made no sense.

She thumbed the speaker and called out to it, "Go away. Shoo."

The wolf dropped back down to four legs, then... and then... its body was changing. Weird movements. The fur receded, showing the wolf's skin. It's front paws changed into hands.

Judy's jaw dropped open. She rubbed her eyes, then looked again. She saw... she actually saw... a wolf snout shrinking until it became a human face, a man's face. Then the wolf's rounded back snapped and bent inward. Towards the stomach. Like a human's spine.

And then... and then... there was a naked man lying in the snow in front of the door.

Stunned, she watched him stand, then pound on the door once more. This time with his hands.

He yelled something she couldn't understand. It sounded familiar. She focused on his long, gray hair...

OMG, it was the old man from Sara's video!

If this was a trick to get her to open the door, it was one heck of a trick. Was she really going to open the door?

But... she couldn't leave a naked man outside in freezing temperatures, could you?

She looked at the other cameras and saw nobody else. Not even more wolves.

Holy bananas!

Did Sara know about him? But... she must. Wouldn't she? Was that why she was so secretive about him?

The man banged again on the door.

Judy took a deep breath and unlocked the three deadbolts, then opened the door.

He came in quickly and closed the latch behind him. He turned to her and froze. It was clear he'd expected to see Sara.

Lola hissed at him then ran and hid. Judy shook herself from her trance and grabbed the blanket from the bed, handing it to him.

Then she made the Hand Talk sign for "Welcome."

His eyes widened, and he made the sign for "greetings."

He... he... was *smelling* her. He took a deep inhale and sniffed! But... she took a shower this morning. Judy turned her head and smelled herself. She did not stink.

Oh, boy.

CHAPTER TWENTY-FIVE

Judy

Judy couldn't stop looking at the old man. The old man with a well muscled, very strong body. The image of him naked stayed in her mind, even as he sat there in a blanket.

The only "old" thing about him was all the loose skin. It hung in folds off his face and loose on his body as though he used to be fat and had lost half his weight. But she thought it was just the effects of time.

A lot of time.

She found him fascinating. And frustrating. He was making Hand Talk signs so fast she couldn't follow, as if Hand Talking was water and he was three days without a drop, as if he'd been dying of thirst.

And... she couldn't focus on that, because he was sitting there naked on her bed in a blanket.

As if she hadn't seen him transform from a wolf into a human just minutes ago.

Maybe the air in the cabin contained a hallucinogen? Was she high?

Because if she wasn't... then sitting not five feet from her was a myth come to life. She was sitting across from an honest-to-god werewolf!

Judy couldn't stay still. She got up and looked around, shook her head, then held out her hand at the man to stop his hand signs. She needed a minute. Heck, she needed an hour.

She needed to take a step back. She had a guest. What do you offer to a guest? She rolled her eyes. Well, some pants would be a start. And food, food was always good.

He was about Sara's height. Where the heck were those disgusting sweat pants of hers? Oh, yeah.

Judy pulled out a pair, turned and held them out to the man.

His eyes crinkled. He'd better not laugh at her!

She dropped them in his lap and turned to the stove. She pulled out two bowls and dished up the stew, then she got two cups and filled them with coffee that had been simmering.

She put the dishes and the cups on the only table in the place and looked back to the man. He'd pulled on the pants and moved to the table.

Judy sat in one chair. He picked up the second chair and looked at it, then sat down across from her. She motioned to the food and he ate. Judy ate as well. It was quiet and very, very normal.

Which she needed right that second.

After the meal, she put their dishes into the sink and decided to start all over. She sat in the chair and faced him, pointing to herself.

"Judy," she said.

He repeated it, then pointed to himself and said something long, with lots of consonants. She shook her head at him.

He again pointed at himself then made the hand signals for "running" and for "wolf."

"Of course you are," she said, then repeated the hand signs. "Running Wolf."

She wanted to talk more with him, a lot more. Maybe the whole day more. But his pounding on the door had seemed urgent.

She made the question sign, pointed to him, then simulated pounding on her door.

He nodded, and formed the sign for "danger."

Oh boy.

CHAPTER TWENTY-SIX

Sara

My phone woke me up in my hotel room at six AM after only four hours of sleep. The sun was shinning bright through a tiny spot at the top of the window where I hadn't sealed the drapes shut.

I decided Alaska could take their 16 hours of daylight this time of year and shove it where the sun don't shine.

I might get a little grouchy when I'm sleep deprived.

Steve and Judy were both on the phone — Steve from Pennsylvania and Judy from my cabin.

I said, "Please tell me you have something. I spent the whole night tracking Connor and getting nothing. He thinks they were toying with him — trying to get him to show his hand."

"What did they do?"

"Shot pool for two hours at the Badger Den at the North Pole, then they took off at midnight in a helicopter and flew 80-something miles to Delta Junction — just to go to another bar. It makes no sense unless they were trying to catch us scrambling to follow or expected us to show up in force."

I carried the phone to the bathroom, stuck my head under the faucet and drank. Then I splashed water on my face.

I felt marginally better, and said, "Judy... that helicopter pilot you got me was stellar."

What I wasn't telling them — what wiped me out — was having to change back and forth from wolf to human too often: wolf to hang around outside the two bars without dying from the cold, and human every time I had to get on the chopper.

"Here's what we've got," Steve said, interrupting my thoughts. "This Neville Huber has been buying up land in Alaska. A lot of land. Some of it under his own name. More of it under some small companies he has, like the Combined Warehousing business you found on the Prince William Sound.

"He's also researching hyper-scale data centers and the use of Alaska's cold weather to off-set the vast amount of heat these places generate. He's got three non-profits working on this — all with names that make them sound like nonprofits that could benefit the Army. Like one that's researching cold weather effects on drone operations.

"But... here's the key about his non-profits — all of them are also buying land in Alaska.

"Among all the businesses and groups he controls, I've found he has over a million acres in Alaska. And he's still buying."

Judy said, "I don't get it. Why?"

I thought. "He could make a fortune offering lower cost locations for A.I. data processing."

Steve added, "Global warming is happening faster than expected. He could be betting that the U.S. coasts will start flooding and the entire South will need ruinous levels of air conditioning just to be habitable. His then-warmer land would jump fifty-fold in value. He'd be sitting pretty."

Judy said, "Remember that guy in Big Sky, Montana? He was living in a rich-person enclave where none of us peons were allowed except as servants. Maybe he wants to wall off an enclave like that in Alaska?"

"Or," I said, musing aloud, "no reason he couldn't have all of these reasons in mind. This would explain the politicians Emil Wissen was touching base with at the dinner Connor went to."

"Yes," Judy said. "They're all in positions to approve even more land purchases for him. Alaska has different boards for sales of private land, state land and federal. Not to mention land for sale at some of the closed military bases up here."

"Okay," I said. "Steve, get us GPS coordinates for his land holdings in very remote areas where nobody could track comings and goings. Then divide them up by location. I'm in Valdez right now and Connor's in Fairbanks. Send each of us the half of the list, whichever we're closest to. I'd like to see how many of these places the two of us can fly over today."

"Anything else?"

"No, get that to us as fast as you can. You can add to each list if you uncover additional locations. Then find us more about this guy. See if knowing his name lets you dig deeper into the Martes holding company."

"On it now." Steve hung up.

"Judy?"

"Uh... yes. What should I do?"

"Are you okay?"

Silence.

"Judy, are you really going crazy there? Do you need to leave?"

"No! I'm fine right here."

I frowned. "No more whining to me about being stuck in the middle of nowhere?"

"I'm okay. What do you need?"

"I assume I can use the same helicopter guy as last night. You have him on retainer?"

"Yes."

"Find a helicopter company out of Fairbanks today for Connor. Put them on retainer too, because we might need them again tomorrow."

"Will do."

I was about to hang up, when I added, "Oh, by the way, once we find Mason — if you're looking for a date, the Valdez boat captain is interested in you."

"Uh... thanks. I'm calling helicopter companies right now." She hung up.

I looked at the dead phone in my hand. What was up with Judy? This was so unlike her.

Maybe she'd been replaced by a pod person, like in those sci-fi movies?

CHAPTER TWENTY-SEVEN

Judy

Judy couldn't decide if today had been the most frustrating day of her life, or the most exciting.

The "trouble" Running Wolf was trying to warn about was hard to pin down. Somebody was killing wolves. That she got.

She understood it was important to him. Being who or what he was. But in the larger scheme of things... killing wolves was legal in Alaska. Couldn't he just stay away from that location?

He seemed to think it would be important to Sara, as well. She couldn't explain to him that Sara was her employer, but she had communicated this house was Sara's and Judy was looking after it for her. He'd nodded vigorously when she showed him a picture of Sara on her phone.

Exactly where these wolf killings were happening was a little harder to pin down. She understood it was a day's travel from this cabin, and by that she clarified he meant wolf travel not human. But how far was that? Googling gave her a ridiculous range, most sites saying wolves travelled 30-40 miles a day, while another claimed up to 100 miles. So probably under 100 miles in any direction. Not that helpful.

Finding out who was killing the wolves was where she struck out. She couldn't find anything online like the sign he made.

And... maybe the problem was her. Every so often while looking at him, her mind flashed back to him transforming from wolf to man and her brain just started bouncing around in her head repeating over and over, *Well, I'll be! Well, I'll be.*

And other times... well... there was something about the man. Something magnetic. She'd be watching him, communicating, when her mind would go blank and she'd just stare at him.

Standing next to him felt funny — he was only three inches taller than her 5'4", but he was strong. Not muscle-pumped strong, but wiry strong. There was no hair on his chest, none at all, which she found somehow... well... her brain had captured a very clear picture of how he looked, naked and pounding on the door. It might be burned on her retinas.

Just how old was the man? Her 50-something years of age, well she must look like a spring chicken to him.

Then there was the way his eyes focused on her, like she had 100% of his attention. It was... unnerving... stimulating.

She wondered how long it had been since he...

Her phone rang.

It was Bill Hanalho, the man who dumped Sara so he could marry within his tribe. Why was he calling...? Oh, of course! She'd sent him the 10-minute video — golly it seemed like years ago — to see if he could translate it.

"You got a minute?" he asked.

"What's up?"

"I think the man in the video was speaking Akitira. It's very close to Lupiti, so I recognized some of the words. I know a man from that tribe who lives nearby, and I have him here with me. He's not fluent in it — there's nobody left who is. Their numbers shrank to just over 400 members after a measles epidemic in the 1890s. They're not even recognized today."

"So what was he saying?"

"Between the two of us, I think we have most of it. It was about the destruction of his people. He was listing the reasons: being forced from their land, starvation, disease. He talked about smallpox wiping out more than half the tribe, which was in the 1830s. Then something else. From his description we think it was about the 1890s measles epidemic. He said the soul, or spirit, of his people died."

"The 1830s?"

"Yes, why?"

"He's sitting right here. Bill — he's never seen a toilet before. I had to show him how it worked. Nor has he seen indoor water."

"Can we talk to him?"

"If he wants to. But... can you ask him something for me? He's been trying to warn me about a place where wolves are being killed. It's very important to him and, for some reason, he thinks Sara has to know as soon as possible. But I can't understand who specifically was killing them and where it is, neither the direction nor the distance."

"We'll try."

Judy turned to Running Wolf, wondering how to explain a telephone.

"I know what to do," she said to Bill. "Call me back using Face-Time. I'll get him on the computer. You'll want to use Hand Talk as well as voice."

Judy shook her head, watching Running Wolf as she set up the computer connection. He'd thought toilets were fascinating, although a little silly, maybe self-indulgent. But it was something else entirely when he saw two native faces on a screen talking to him in voice and sign. He'd looked behind the screen, then turned toward Judy.

"Far away from here," she'd hand signed to him.

He'd nodded, thoughtfully, then turned back to the screen.

For the next hour, the three men forgot about her as they navigated their way to understanding each other.

She must have fallen into a trance, listening to their voices as they spoke words she couldn't understand. She was jolted when Running Wolf suddenly stood up, pushed the screen away from him, gave her the strangest look, then opened the door to the cabin and walked out.

Judy ran to the camera covering the front of the cabin and saw him strip off the sweats and transform back to wolf, then run away.

Numbly, she stepped outside and picked up the clothes, then re-locked the door bolts.

She moved the screen back around to face her. Lola came over and jumped into her lap. Judy petted her.

She asked the two men on the computer, "What happened?"

They looked at each other, but neither talked.

"Well?"

Bill said, "He found out how few of his people were left."

Judy glared at them. "Why would you tell him that?"

Bill shook his head. "We couldn't hide it. He wanted to speak to their shaman. We had to tell him that they no longer had one. Then he wanted to speak to someone more fluent than Jordan here. We had to tell him Jordan is the best that remains."

Judy closed her eyes.

Bill said, "Then he asked how many of his people still exist..."

"That's when he left?"

"Yes."

"Oh my gosh." Judy's eyes felt wet and she rubbed them. Hard.

Bill said, "At least we got you the location where someone is killing wolves. You want it?"

Judy grabbed a paper and pen. "Tell me."

CHAPTER TWENTY-EIGHT

Sara

At about 10 PM that night I stumbled into Connor's hotel room at the Springhill Suites Marriott in Fairbanks, carrying four Starbucks' Ventis — two coffees for him and two macha tea lattes for me.

We had each spent ten hours in the air searching for likely hideouts — Connor from Fairbanks south and me from Anchorage north.

Neville Huber had a lot of property. Some of it was in residential areas. Well... Alaska's idea of residential areas, which was more rustic than, say, anywhere else in the U.S. He owned — or controlled through a company or nonprofit — some single lots hidden among other lots, and more where he'd scarfed up adjoining plots.

We'd ignored both of those types of holdings. Instead we looked for more isolated land, with no roads and no neighbors. Especially lots where nobody else could see a plane land on his property.

Connor had investigated six in his area. One looked especially good, except his infrared detector told him nobody was currently there. We might have to go back there, but for now we had a better lead.

One of the locations on my list of five was an abandoned Nike

Hercules missile site, which was purchased 15 years ago by one of Huber's nonprofits — one whose stated mission was researching "improved military operations in cold weather venues." This site showed two heat signatures inside and, depending on how deep it went, there could be more. We'd check it out first.

Judy did some quick research on it that she sent us. She'd found eight "official" Nike Hercules sites in Alaska that were built in the late 1950s. At the time, they each held nuclear missile batteries designed to intercept and shoot down incoming nukes launched from the USSR. Five of those sites were near Fairbanks and three were near Anchorage. All were decommissioned in the late 1970s. All eight of these sites were next to still-active military bases, — so we eliminated them.

The location that attracted us was a ninth missile site set up as a secret last-chance fallback in case Fairbanks and Anchorage were both taken out in a first strike.

Test Site 9 was in the middle of nowhere, about 90 miles southeast of Fairbanks and an equal number of miles northeast of Anchorage. Its isolation made it almost impossible to sabotage, but they'd had to rotate soldiers and staff in and out of there as soldiers reportedly hated it. There was nowhere to go in their off hours.

The place was no longer a secret by the time it was decommissioned in 1976, but it was never officially put on the books. The Army buried it until retired Colonel Huber asked to buy it for his cold weather military research nonprofit.

"Okay, everybody," I said once all four of us were on the call. "Good work all. Judy - thanks for finding me a last-minute room here, so I won't have to find out if Connor snores."

"I don't snore," Connor said.

I rolled my eyes at him.

"The biggest problem is we'll be attacking a defended position with an unknown number of hostiles and, hopefully, vulnerable hostages there. Connor tells me it's suicide for just two people."

He broke in. "I just called two friends of mine to come join the fun. They'll be here tomorrow morning. I'm sending a charter plane for them so they can bring their own weapons."

"What size are they?" Judy asked. "I assume they need full cold-weather gear including breathers with heat-exchangers? The same I sent you and Sara yesterday?"

"Yes, full gear. To be safe, assume two sizes up from mine for one guy and my size for the other. Better too big than too small."

"Okay," she said. "I got your text about what we're paying them."

"How are we coming on the snowmobiles?" I asked.

Judy said, "This part was fun. They had what we needed in Fairbanks, but I had to pay a fortune for them — double the list price for everything. The cargo plane to get them to Cantwell is on top of that. The owner feels sorry for me, thinks I'm working for a 'rich bitch' with more money than brains, who likes to show off for her guests."

I laughed. "Gee thanks."

"So he said he might be willing to buy some of them back after your vacation. For a used price, of course."

My eyebrows rose, then settled back down. "Good. Tell him he can screw me on the resale as much he'd like because you don't care. That way it shouldn't dawn on him we might be using them for something different — like an assault."

"I already told him he could!"

"I should have known," I said. "Okay, let's all get some sleep tonight. We'll regroup about mid-day. I want to be at the target site ready to enter around midnight tomorrow.

"Connor, I know you've told me 1 AM is best for attacking, but it'll only be dark from 11 PM to 4:30 AM. Should we wait until one or go at midnight?"

"Let's go at midnight," he said. "We might need an extra hour of darkness to get out of there."

"Sara?" Judy said. "I need to talk to you privately, when you get to your room."

I raised my eyebrows and took a look at the room key I'd been given. I was on the same floor as Connor. "Okay, call me in five minutes." Then I hung up and left for my room.

When she called, Judy said, "This probably won't affect your mission, but you should know there are men killing wolves in that general area, most likely right at the missile site."

I froze. I couldn't even breathe. *Why was she talking to me about wolves?*

"Why would I need to know that?"

"Running Wolf said you needed to know immediately."

"Running Wolf?"

"Oh, my," Judy said, with a huge sigh. "I got a lot you need to know. Running Wolf is the Native American guy you sent me the tape of. You told me to get it translated."

I took a breath. Maybe it wasn't so bad. "He said that on the tape?"

There was an even bigger sigh from her. "No. It wasn't on the tape. The man came back. That's when he told me."

This wasn't making sense. "He came back? You let him in the cabin?"

"Well, I wasn't leaving a naked man outside to freeze to death."

"Naked?"

"Don't you play games with me, Missy. I know you know exactly what the man is — or you wouldn't have been so paranoid about who I got to translate him. You told me, and I quote, 'make damn sure no translator reveals a word of what he said.'"

I tried to say something, but nothing came out. Probably because I had no clue what to say. Did this mean she knows about him — but not about me? What in the...

"Wait," I said. "Who'd you get to translate?"

I heard another sigh. "You're not going to like this."

"So far," I said through gritted teeth, "I haven't liked a single word you've said. So you might as well keep it coming."

"I called Bill Hanalho," she said, then her voice became squeaky, "Don't shoot me. I told him I hated him on your behalf."

I dropped onto the bed, the phone falling from my hand. I shook my head and barked out a laugh, then squelched it.

Sure, let's toss in my recent ex into this mess.

I picked the phone back up and said, "When did all this happen? Why are you just telling me now?"

"I called Bill back when you first sent me the tape. I figured he could best tell us who to get as a translator who could keep a secret. He was my best bet since Mason wasn't around to ask."

I nodded to myself. It was a good call on her part. "And when did — Running Wolf's his name?"

"Yes."

"When did he arrive?"

"Yesterday morning."

"About the time you stopped whining about wanting to leave the cabin?"

"Uh... about then. Yes."

"How did you talk to him?"

"Bill suggested he might be using Plains Indian Sign Language, so whenever I had some free time, I opened YouTube and learned it."

"Of course you did." I shook my head and smiled. "So... only you and Bill know about Running Wolf?"

"No... one other person. Although I think he only knows about the man — not his other... form? Bill figured out Running Wolf was probably Akitira due to the language similarities with Lupiti, so he called me with one of the few people left who can speak any of that language. A guy named Jordan."

"Judy, is Running Wolf still at the cabin?" *Had he stayed two days and a night?*

"No, he walked right out the door a couple of hours ago, right after they told him there were less than 400 people left from his tribe."

I took a deep breath. "We'll talk more about this later. But I'm asleep on my feet right now, so give me the short version about our target missile site."

"He was near there with some wolves. Regular wolves, not like him. There were two guys with rifles. He made sure we knew they were rifles that could fire without reloading. They shot at his group and killed one of the wolves. That's what he wanted to tell you."

"Okay," I said. "We'll talk later. Right now I have to put it out of my mind and get some badly needed sleep before tomorrow's mission."

"Goodnight, Sara."

I hit the button, then flung myself back on the bed and looked at the ceiling. My mind was churning, but I needed to sleep.

Ever since I was turned... ever since I started taking on monsters to rescue people... I've had trouble getting to sleep. My solution was to take one milligram of Melatonin at night. It was just enough to quiet the "what-ifs" in my head, but not enough to give me weird, vivid dreams.

The way my life was going, I had all the weird and vivid I could handle. I didn't need more in my sleep.

However, I reached in my bag and pulled out the bottle and threw five of them in my mouth. I would never sleep without them. I'd take the strange dreams tonight in order to get the sleep.

CHAPTER TWENTY-NINE

Mason

Mason took a deep breath and tried to hide his shaking hands. He'd done it. Repercussions would come — the only question was how soon.

He'd dithered for too long as it was. Contacting Sara meant they'd get here faster, which also meant Emma, and probably him, would die faster. But once he finished with the three names Felix had given him, they'd both die anyway.

What had settled his mind was realizing Sara could show up any day. Any minute now. If she didn't know how many people were here, she might come alone or just with Connor. They'd be terribly outnumbered, and no matter how good both of them were, they would likely die, too. He had to warn her.

Businesswoman Aurora Padgitt was the third person Felix's hackers couldn't find dirt on. Now it was up to him.

Padgitt took an annual vacation to Cancun, Mexico, but Mason hadn't found any bank accounts for her there. However, Belize was just a short one-and-a-half-hour plane hop away, and Mason bet more than one visitor to Cancun took that ride under an alias. Belize was one of the top five countries in the world where white-collar-criminals could hide their loot.

Mason had posted queries to two hacker forums about the best banks in the Caribbean for hiding money from U.S. taxes. He'd also tagged some individual hacker IDs with the question as well. This was all what his captors would expect.

What he hoped they didn't expect was that one of the hacker IDs he'd tagged — SwordMaster — was an alias for his friend and former roommate, Steve Callahan.

To all five of the hackers, he'd added some personal comments. To one he asked how that summer project of his was coming. He congratulated another on finding a vulnerability that sent Microsoft scrambling. To his friend's alias, he said, "Remember our joint project from three years ago? I think you had a source at a Belize bank. Need advice on where to start for tax-hidden funds."

With each message he included a picture of a little boy giving the middle-finger salute.

In Steve's picture, he'd embedded a hidden doc in the jpeg file.

He hoped like hell it would alert Steve to find the doc. The only joint project they'd worked on three years ago was when Steve helped Sara locate Mason.

In the document, he'd given Steve his GPS location, and told him that the place had 8-10 armed mercenaries at any time, that Emma was on the third level up from the bottom (he had no clue how many more levels up it went), and that their orders were to kill Emma immediately if there was a rescue attempt.

He'd added they would need medical help for Emma, who was newly missing a hand. "No innocents here," he'd said. He didn't want Sara risking her life trying not to kill people who deserved to die.

As every damn one of them did.

He'd done what he could. Maybe more than he should.

He got back responses on two Belize banks, and he started running programs to break into their records.

An hour later, one of the forums pinged with a reply from Steve, aka SwordMaster. "No time now. If u can wait 24-26, might have something. You'll owe me — I want that facial recog program you developed."

Since Mason had already given Steve his facial recognition program, he knew he'd found the embedded document.

Mason turned back to his other programs. *Oh god. Twenty-four hours and then what? We're both dead?*

CHAPTER THIRTY

Sara

How do you hide a military assault, when you've got three guys the size of houses carrying huge duffle bags clanking with equipment? Not to mention eight top-of-the-line snowmobiles.

Steve broke the news that he'd heard from Mason last night. The intel Mason sent was both great and terrible... great in that he and Emma were alive... great that the GPS he sent was right where we thought they were.

But... if there was a way to go through 10 armed men in a fortified building without making noise... well, I didn't know it. Nor did Connor.

Also, we couldn't question anyone locally about the site. Mason's captors were bound to have contacts in at least one "nearby" town.

Our target GPS spot was 150 miles from Anchorage, which meant neither we nor our snowmobiles were flying there direct by helicopter.

The closest airport to where we needed to be was Cantwell, a town of 117 people, where the guy working part-time at the airport probably had the entire town on speed dial. The next closest was Glennallen, with a few hundred more people. Glennallen was 315 miles southeast of Cantwell — on the opposite side of the former missile site.

In between was pretty much nothing — except our target.

Judy split our operations between the two tiny cities so we looked less like an army. She'd had four electric snowmobiles flown hanging from helicopters out of Glennallen last night. They were dropped about 30 miles from our target. The four gas-powered snowmobiles were flown out of Cantwell, and dropped off about 60 miles from our target.

I was most worried about the men in our group. I'd told Connor to do everything he could to make himself and his men look like vacationers instead of an invading army.

Special-ops men — as long as they're dressed in very loose, casual clothes and don't have a buzz haircut — *can* look like overweight civilians. If they tone down the cocky attitude. A huge "if."

I had my fingers crossed.

We met at my suite at the Captain Cook in Anchorage.

Judy bought each of them yellow Dior backpacks ($3000+) as well as Prada after-ski boots ($1800),and ski goggles ($800) with their distinctive orange color. But rich-people designers weren't making snowsuits in giant-guy sizes. For that, the men needed their military-issue snow-camo suits. The blatant accessories would hopefully help hide their military purpose here.

Connor knew both of the men from previous operations, but this was the first I'd met them.

Danny Fry had a face that looked surprisingly like Volodymyr Zelenskyy, the President of Ukraine, but was a foot taller and weighed an extra 100 pounds. He was just slightly smaller than Connor — which is to say he was huge.

Marko Smit, on the other hand, dwarfed Connor and was a startling sight. His gleaming bald head was covered with tattoos of eagles. Anybody who saw him would think he'd come to kill them — nobody would see him as a vacationer. I was very happy Judy had sent Northwoods, fur-trapper hats for the men. I was surprised she'd been able to find one big enough for him.

From the way Marko refused to look at me when we met, I knew immediately he'd be a problem.

I gave them the cover story Judy had developed — we were pretending that I was a rich bitch with more money than brains who liked to show off for her guests. Marko snorted in amusement at the "rich bitch."

Photos of Mason were handed out as well as ones of Emma.

I advised the team about the noise problem we had. That according to Mason, Emma would be killed at the first sign of a rescue attempt. I explained we were looking at probably 10 armed men.

Our first goal was to get close to the place without being discovered — which is why the last 30 miles would be via electric snowmobiles. Worse case, I told them I'd walk in myself, blind, and communicate intel back to them.

"I'm in charge of the operation — so if I say 'fire' or 'stop firing' that's what happens."

Marko looked down but I could see him rolling his eyes.

I added, "But... Connor knows much more than me about assaults, so he's in minute-to-minute command. What he says goes, unless I countermand him."

My phone buzzed, and I saw it was Judy. I stepped away from the group to answer it.

"Y'all got a complication," she said.

"What?"

"Running Wolf came back here. I told him we were attacking the site where his wolf was killed. That they had hostages we had to rescue."

I waited, but she didn't volunteer any more. "And?"

Judy sighed. "And he told me that he and his wolves would join the fight. To help us and to make them pay for Snow Dancer."

"Snow Dancer?"

"I think that was the name he'd given the wolf that was shot. He said... he thinks they can draw the men out of the bunker, so you can get them."

I thought. That was actually a good idea. But... the complications! "You couldn't talk him out of it?"

"No. He told me, then left. He said they'd be there by dark. That's when you were planning to launch, so at least his timing is good."

"Thanks," I said and hung up.

I walked back over to the men.

"Update," I said. "We're getting some help. I know a guy who commands a pack of wolves. They're going to start the battle for us by drawing some men out of the bunker. They're going to howl, draw out as many men as they can, and we'll be waiting to take them down with knives. No noise."

Marko rolled his eyes. "Wolves? Come on."

"Yes, wolves. The men there killed one of their pack a few days ago. They've decided to help us rescue our friends."

Marko sneered. "Wolves."

I nodded. I doubted he cared about wolves. He was using them to show his contempt for me as the leader of this group. I was glad to get the challenge now, before it could threaten our lives."

I said, "You hard of hearing, Marko?"

Connor shoved his shoulder. "I told you, she's the leader."

"Sure she is. After all, she can talk to wolves." He looked at me. "They got their own language? Two yips means yes? Or?"

I shoved his shoulder. He was up lightning fast and took a step towards me. I had to turn up my face or my eyes would have been level with his collar bone.

This man wouldn't react to reason. He wouldn't care how smart I was, or how well I could help protect the team. He believed power came from physical strength. It had worked for him all his life, and he wasn't changing for me.

I was a little less cocky about my strength these days. The mercenary who'd escaped my car up near Wasilla had shown me, for the first time, that the strength I'd gained from my transformation had its limits.

But... if I couldn't beat Marko, I could still shock him.

I smiled at him. "Tough guy, huh?"

He smiled back.

"How long do you think it would take to beat me in arm wrestling?"

He sneered. "About a second. But it would probably crack your wrist. Maybe even your arm."

I widened my smile. "A second, huh? Big talk for a big man. But..." I looked him up and down, considering. "I'll bet you couldn't do it in five seconds."

"Don't be ridiculous."

Connor was frowning at me. "Sara?"

I turned back to Marko. "Let's give it a try. If you can beat me in under five seconds, you can report to Connor instead of me. But if you can't — if it takes you more than five seconds — then you shut the hell up, take my orders, and do the damn job I hired you for."

I stared hard at him, although I knew my glare lost a lot of its force because I had to look up so far to see him. "Deal?"

Danny had been watching our interaction. I saw his eyebrows wrinkle, then he turned and looked at Connor. I made a mental note to myself about Danny's ability to read people. He'd done it to me, and knew I expected to win the bet, so he was looking to Connor to see how that was possible.

But Connor was just looking at me, puzzled. He'd seen me fight and knew I was strong — at least for a female. Clearly he thought I must have some trick up my sleeve.

Marko had been silent.

"Deal?"

He nodded. "Deal."

I hadn't arm wrestled anyone since I was a little kid, so I hadn't anticipated the problem of two people trying it when one had a forearm about eight inches shorter than the other. We had to put the hotel's Giddeon bible and two pillows under my elbow so we could grasp hands.

Connor stood over us and held our clasped hands. He looked at me, giving me a chance to back out. I just smiled and nodded.

"On three," he said and counted down.

Holy crap the guy was strong! The description of Superman popped into my head — that he could "bend steel in his bare hands."

Marko probably could, too.

He pushed my arm half way down in the first second, but he must have eased off a fraction when he thought victory was assured. Quickly, I pushed both our hands back up — not all the way up, but up. His eyes widened, his frown got fierce, and he strained harder.

I gave it everything I had. I held us without moving for at least two seconds before he started making headway. Slowly... slowly... he moved my arm down.

"Five seconds!" called Connor. I grinned at the surprise in his voice.

Then I bared my teeth at Marko, as he gradually, inch by inch, moved my arm down until the back of my wrist hit the table.

"Time?" I asked.

"Nine seconds," Connor said.

It felt like my knuckles were pulverized, but I was able to — discretely — move my fingers, so I figured I was okay. My forearm felt like a truck ran over it.

Marko looked very confused. "How'd you do that?" There was no heat behind the words — he really wanted to know.

"I'm stronger than I look." I shrugged my shoulders, then I held out my hand to shake his. "So, Marko, are we good?"

He turned to Connor who lifted his shoulders in an "I don't have a clue" shrug.

Marko took my hand. "I'm good if you tell me how you did that."

"After the mission. Now, about the wolves...."

I took a deep breath. "The wolves are on our team. The more men they can draw out who want to shoot at them, the better our odds. Plus shooting at wolves won't raise any alarms inside the bunker. With their help we can be inside the place before anyone notices. If you see a wolf, point your guns away from them. It will differentiate you from the bad guys shooting at them. Do not under any circumstances point a gun at a wolf. Any questions, or are we clear?"

Danny cleared his throat. "If one of them attacks me..."

I looked at him. His foot was bouncing around. Wolves made him nervous.

I raised a finger at him. "*If* you are pointing your gun away from them, none of this pack will attack you. I guarantee it. And if you kill a wolf who isn't right at your throat — I will kill you."

Three pairs of eyes shot to me in outrage and their mouths opened in unison to protest.

Quietly, so they had no doubt as to how serious I was, I said, "I *will* kill you even if I have to hunt you down to do it. The wolves are under my protection. We. Do. Not. Kill. Our. Allies."

Their mouths closed, but they clearly didn't like this.

I said, "If any of you can't abide by this, you can leave now. Each wolf is a volunteer member of this team. They're not getting paid, yet they are risking their lives right along with us."

"Okay by me," said Danny, but he felt compelled to add, "I guess."

The other two men nodded agreement.

"I'm hoping we get to see them before the shooting starts, so they can smell each of you. Then they'll recognize you as allies, and you can learn to see them the same way."

Oh, my. If I could only get a photo of the looks on their faces!

Instead, we grabbed our bags and left for the airport.

CHAPTER THIRTY-ONE

Sara

Connor and I made sure all the weapons were hidden before we got off the puddle-jumper single-engine plane in Cantwell. There, I played my rich-bitch role in a fancy white snowsuit, giving each of the men air kisses and treating our helicopter pilots there as if they were my servants.

I hoped the local at the airport, as well as the pilots, viewed us as idiots instead of nefarious people that they needed to report to Alaska's Wildlife Troopers.

We'd hired two choppers because we needed to transport 900 pounds of men, plus me and two pilots, not to mention about 800 pounds of weapons and ammo hidden inside huge dufflebags. Added in were 64 pounds of lithium batteries.

I would have loved to take the helicopters all the way to the electric snowmobiles, but if the bad guys had any kind of lookout at the old missile site, that would be the first thing they'd listen for. Noise from helicopters or snowmobiles that were 30-40 miles away would not be a problem — as long as they didn't come closer.

It was about 10 PM when the pilots dropped us where our E-10 powered snowmobiles were waiting. The sun was hitting the tops of several mountains, so we had an hour before it turned dark.

After the helicopters left, the three men opened the dufflebags and some of the arsenal of weapons started disappearing into white camouflage suits and snowmobiles. More stayed in the bags that were loaded onto the snowmobiles.

When everything was ready, I checked the GPS coordinates to where our electric snowmobiles were waiting.

I said, "If any of you feel the need to rev engines and speed, do it now so you get it out of your system. Once we're five minutes from here, we need to run as quietly as we can. We're taking these snowmobiles within 30 miles of our target. You each have four batteries for the electric snowmobiles, but between the cold that drains them and the high speed we might need to get away, I couldn't risk extending the range any farther than that.

"Noise travels out here, and we need surprise. So run these as quietly as you can."

"After five minutes," insisted Marko.

I smiled. "Yes, after five."

Danny and Marko both took off, racing. I smirked and turned to Connor. "You have the signal jammer?"

He patted a bag strapped on the front of his ride. "It's right there." Then he took off with a whoop, chasing the other two.

I, of course, took off at a sedate, well-controlled speed.

Okay, maybe not. Girls wanna have fun too.

"Quiet as possible" was not at all, so I was relieved when we reached the electric vehicles, right where they were supposed to be.

We quickly bagged up all the loud-colored designer accessories used to make us look more like tourists. We moved weapons and operational gear to the electric snowmobiles, put in the first batteries, and left for our next stop. It was two miles from the target, and in a valley where a partial overhang would hide us from it.

As we neared the location, I veered off to a nearby site I'd studied on Google Earth. It was a small, flat area behind a natural rock face. I used the spot to drop off a special bag I'd packed with a warm set of clothes, boots and hat, as well as vacuum-sealed packs of salmon, just in case I found myself in either wolf or naked-human form and needed to transform.

I joined the others after that and we packed weapons and ammo onto our bodies.

There was a light breeze I could barely feel under my face mask and I inhaled frequently, sniffing the air. Until I smelled wolf.

I touched the shoulders of all three men to get their attention. "No guns," I reminded them.

I turned in the direction of the scent and saw gray fur behind a tree trunk. I walked towards it.

I could tell that it was Running Wolf. He walked toward me, his eyes staying on the three men. I watched them as well, kneeling down to greet the wolf.

Running Wolf shoved his snout against my face in a typical wolf greeting. I reached around and hugged him. Wolves don't much care for it — they feel trapped — but his human side recognized the gesture. He pushed back and toppled me down onto my back. Then he stood over me.

Oh no you don't, I thought, with a smile. I stood up, held his body and swung a leg over him. Two could play this dominance game.

His mouth opened in a grin, tongue hanging down, and he moved away from me. Once again he stared at the three men and looked back at me. I nodded.

He yipped, and eight white wolves materialized out of nowhere. With their pure white arctic coats, they could hide much better than Running Wolf — whose gray coat was better suited for life in the Great Plains.

They surrounded me and stuck their noses up against me. I unzipped the front of my suit to give them a better smell.

Then I turned and walked, slowly, towards the three men. I must have been a sight with nine wolves prancing around in circles, surrounding me. Danny and Marko gaped.

Connor was watching me with much too thoughtful an expression.

I realized the scene was reminiscent of when I'd protected him from another pack of wolves in Yellowstone — except I was in wolf form then. I did not want him to think about the parallels.

I walked straight to Danny and took his right arm in mine and squeezed it. I could hear his heartbeat, which was much faster than normal. He was breathing harder as well.

"Open your suits so they can get a better whiff," I said to the men.

Connor and Marko were nervous, but not really scared. Very curious.

Danny was giving off the stink of fear sweat. I walked him a couple of steps away and said, "This is good. Your... adrenaline is running high." I'd barely stopped myself from saying "fear." "You want them to recognize your smell with the adrenalin."

In reality, the smell of fear draws wolves. Dogs too. They both know not to trust humans who have it because they can be dangerous. I wanted the wolves to know this was a normal smell for Danny. Normal, that is, whenever he was around wolves. I didn't want them to see him as a threat.

Scents acquired, I moved with the wolves slightly away from the men. I pulled out my phone and cued up a video that Judy had sent me earlier. She used Hand Talk to ask Running Wolf to wait until my men had snuck up close to the target, so they could use knives to quietly take out anyone who came out to shoot the wolves.

I showed the video to Running Wolf. He watched it, then nodded at me.

Holding a finger up, I cued a second video. In it, Judy told him not to get too close. To stay far enough away and move fast enough to protect him and the others. She told him that we didn't want anyone else to die.

When the second video finished, he turned his head aside. His human side apparently wanted revenge for his pack mate. I did *not* want him to be rash — to take too big a risk.

Gently, I took his head in my hands and turned it toward me. Then I rubbed my right palm in a circular motion on my chest. I'd asked Judy how to sign the word "please."

He stared at me, then ran to his wolves and they disappeared into the snow-covered trees.

I came back to the men, who were looking at me as if I were an alien, as if I were spouting antennas out the top of my head.

"Let's take as long as we need to get up there without being seen. If they've got warning systems that we miss, and it all goes loud, get down inside as fast as possible to rescue Mason and Emma."

It had seemed so easy on Google Earth, a three-mile uphill walk with scrub bushes and huge rocks breaking up the snow. The first mile cured me of that. We were still below a rise, hidden from their view, but the footing was unsure.

The former missile site had been reduced to a single above-ground building — maybe 50-by-15 feet. Two doors were on one long side of the building. The other three had no doors, windows, or anything else.

We were planning to go into both doors at the same time, so Connor and Danny were crawling up the slope to one of the small, 15-foot sides, while Marko and I were crawling up the opposite side of the hill.

Thank god I was never in the military. Following Connor's lead, we were all four slithering on our bellies, looking for indents that could be mine placements or trip wires.

I always thought men were more impatient than women, but Marko seemed just fine. After 15 minutes, I hated it. After 30, I wanted to jump up, scream and run around in circles.

I hit my mic on a channel that was just connected to Connor. "You all did this in the military?" I asked. "I'm going to be too old to fight by the time we get there."

"Your choice, darlin'," he drawled. It was never a good sign when Connor broke out his otherwise-hidden Tennessee drawl. "Too old or too dead to fight. You pick."

"Funny," I grumbled, inching along like a worm.

Also... I felt like a mummy. I always did when I went out into the Alaskan winter. All the clothes, the layers, the heated face masks, the goggles — I looked like the Michelin man... which was okay back at my cabin, but not here.

Here I was going after bad guys. Trying to rescue my friend and his girl. I was going to fight, damnit, in a full Michelin-man outfit? If I ran into someone, I might just bounce off him.

And... what if I needed to transform? Would my wolf be trapped in all these clothes?

There had been a mild wind blowing for what seemed like the 14 hours we'd been crawling up this hill. But, in an instant, the wind got serious. It came out of nowhere, hard and fast, and it picked up snow from the ground and threw it with force right into our faces.

Suddenly I could see nothing — not even Marko who had been crawling 15 feet from my side.

"Excellent," I heard Connor say in my earbud on the channel we were all linked to. "Worse visibility for them, but harder for us to spot traps."

I felt a touch at the back of my neck and nearly screamed. I turned and saw Running Wolf beside me. I took extra breaths to slow my heart back down, then hit the mic and told the group, "I have a wolf with me now, so he can alert the others once we're ready."

Amazingly, Marko and I reached our side of the building without anything going wrong. Five seconds later, Connor reported over the mic that he and Danny were in place.

The visibility was a little better here at the top of this hill. Maybe there wasn't as much snow to blow. I darted my head around our corner of the building and back. I could see our door about 18 feet down, and Connor's and Danny's door 10 feet past that.

I nodded to Running Wolf and he disappeared into the blowing snow. "The wolves are being alerted," I said into my mic.

Soon, wolf howls echoed around us. Multiple voices. Multiple songs. Somehow combining into the most beautiful music ever created.

There was a blur, and I heard loud claw marks scraping metal. *The doors! No!*

I looked around our corner of the building and saw a flash of gray fur as Running Wolf finished scratching the far door, then ran off disappearing from view. Another male with more balls than common sense. I wanted to wring his neck. Why can't everyone I care about just stay safe, so I can stop worrying about them?

The howling got louder. It cut right through the wind as if it were a knife cutting through smoke. Like the wind didn't even exist.

I heard a metal clang.

Connor's voice rang in my ears. "Do not shoot. Wait until we have the most men outside that will come. I'll say when, but it will be when it looks like they're going back inside."

Two men came out the door on Connor's side. Both had serious-looking rifles.

Connor said in my ear, "They've got FN SCARs."

Marko nodded, so that meant something to the others. It made me realize how completely out of my element I was here.

One of the targets stopped about 10 feet from the door and was listening to the howls, trying to triangulate. Fortunately, wolf howls bounce around more than words, making it much harder to identify their location.

The other man walked towards the side of the building where Connor and Danny were waiting, then turned the corner.

A minute later, "One down," was whispered in my ear. I was relieved I hadn't heard any noise from the takedown.

Was nobody coming out the door nearest me and Marko?

The man out front fired his rifle. I winced, hoping he didn't hit any of the wolves.

He taped his throat and his mouth started moving. He must be on a comms system himself.

Suddenly the other door — the one closest to me — opened and another man stepped out. He had a rifle over his shoulder, and his hands were holding a pair of binoculars. He said something to the man who'd fired, and they both laughed.

Connor's voice said in our ears. "Marko. Danny. Each of you take the guy closest to you on my count. Knives only. No shooting. Three. Two. One."

I saw Marko sneak up behind his target, then both hostiles drop.

We ran to our respective doors.

"Re-look at the photos," said Connor, as we all stripped off our face re-breathers and gloves, stashing them inside our snow suits.

Connor said, "Rules of engagement. Kill only if you have to. That includes everyone inside except Mason and Emma. And be quiet. As long as we can."

Rifles were slung over shoulders, while knives and silenced pistols came out. I joined them.

We nodded at each other, then Danny and Marko each grabbed the door closest to them and — guns leading — slipped inside. I watched Connor follow Danny in, then I went in my door after Marko.

CHAPTER THIRTY-TWO

Sara

A wall blocked me from seeing the other team's entrance. Marko and I were in a computer monitoring station with three empty chairs. Four of the eight screens showed vast snowy expanses... no wait... on one screen I saw a white wolf moving out of the view.

I glanced at Marko, who was staring at me. Annoyed. He pointed his head towards an open doorway, the only other exit from this room.

Ah, yes, clear the rooms first.

As we put our backs against either side of the open door, we heard another one close, along with the sound of a toilet flushing. A short man in white camouflage pants and a black t-shirt came strolling through the door, displaying arms built through a ton of gym workouts.

Marko slammed the butt of his rifle hard into the side of the guy's head and he dropped to the floor. I bent down and fastened his hands and feet with zip ties. Then I cut off most of the front of his t-shirt and shoved it in his mouth and slapped duct tape around his head, covering his mouth.

Noise made me jerk my head up to look at the door, where Marko was already greeting Connor and Danny.

Connor set the signal jammer. Now nobody could contact rein-forcements.

I ran back to the security monitors. The four screens showing inside rooms didn't reveal what I wanted them to: three were focused on hallways and one showed an empty cell.

I needed Mason!

Danny grabbed a chair and rolled it in front of the system, shoving me away.

"He's our best for security systems," Connor told me.

"How many floors are there?" I asked. "Because Mason said Emma is on the third from the lowest."

Danny had pulled out a drawer with schematics and codes for the cameras. "Five. So two floors down."

Connor asked, "Sets of stairs? Elevator?"

"Main stairs are in the center, with another set in the back. No elevator."

Danny had been moving the cameras, scanning hallways and finding men in camouflage.

"How many men?"

"Six more so far, but there are three doors off a hall on the floor below that I can't see into. I'm guessing it's for the brass, so assume at least one there. Maybe more."

I asked, "No Mason or Emma?"

"Not yet."

I looked at Connor. "What else is on this floor?"

"Abandoned old monitoring stations with knobs and dials. Probably the old Ajax missile launch control stations. Nobody's there."

Danny said, "Next floor down has offices and mess hall — and two men."

"Which stairs are they facing or closest to?" I asked.

"The back stairs."

I nodded at Connor. "You two go down those and wait. I'll go down the main stairs and create a distraction." Marko's eyebrows raised so high they might have hit his hairline, if he'd had one.

I put my snow hat into an inside pocket then holstered my suppressed Colt 1911. I unzipped my snowsuit and fluffed out my hair.

I was counting on them not shooting an unarmed female on sight. Particularly if they'd been stuck in this hole for a few days.

Marko said, "It won't work with these guys. They're pros. They'll shoot you on sight."

I looked at him. "You willing to bet $10 on that?"

Marko shook his head. "You're betting your life. But I'll take your $10."

Marko didn't know I was only betting my pain, not my life. I tapped my mike. "Danny, tell them when the men turn and start coming towards me."

Connor nodded and motioned for Marko to go with him.

The steps were concrete so I didn't worry about making noise. I went down, hit the landing, then turned for the final steps into a small eating area with five tables, chairs, and a buffet area for food. Behind that, I could see a kitchen.

Nobody was in sight.

"Danny?" I asked quietly into my mike.

"I can see you. Door to your left is a bathroom, kitchen and food storage ahead. The two men are to your right in the hallway that leads to offices. They might be talking to someone, but I can't see in the offices."

"Connor?" I asked.

"Got it."

I laid my rifle down on the steps. Then I took a deep breath, and said loudly, "Who's a girl gotta fuck to get a sandwich in this joint?"

Both my empty hands were held out in appeal as I walked towards the kitchen, looking around in exasperation.

Two huge men in white camouflage pants and tight t-shirts came running out of the hall, their rifles pointing at me.

"Who the hell are you?" one of them said.

I turned my upraised hands to them and twisted my wrists back and forth. "Really, guys. This is some crap reception you've got going."

That was the last of the "clever" comments I could come up with, so I was delighted to see Connor and Marko come up and hit them from behind. Both men crumpled to the floor. Connor and Marko kicked their rifles towards me and pocketed their handguns and knives. They were applying zip ties as I ran past them.

"No third man?" I asked.

Connor shook his head.

"I didn't clear the restroom."

Marko looked at me like I was an idiot. I raised my hands. "Sorry, you can't pay me enough to check out a men's bathroom."

He stalked off to check it himself, but I'm almost sure he was suppressing a smile.

There were three offices leading off the hall, but they were small and vacant — no men, not even hiding under desks.

Connor watched me, then Marko joined him.

I pointed at Marko and said, "You owe me $10."

"Worth it," he said. "Even I might have looked before shooting after that comment."

I tapped my hands on the walls in the room. Concrete block, like all the other walls here. "I don't like it. Danny, which room were the guys standing outside of?"

His voice in our ears said, "Close to where Connor is standing now."

That could only be this office or the one next to it. I moved to the second office but again — no man. No papers sat on the desk, but there was a coffee mug with some dregs in it. I stuck my index finger into the cup.

"It's still warm."

A fire-alarm-loud buzzer sounded, making all three of us jump.

"Intruder alert..." blared out from somewhere. "Plan Omega... Intruder alert... Plan Omega."

Connor said, "Shit — so much for stealth. Danny? Back stairs?"

"Two coming up the front stairs. One from the back."

I said, "I'll take the back. You two take the front." And I ran.

Damnit! Mason said they'd kill Emma if there was a rescue attempt. If she dies... No time to do this the safe way...

I grabbed the door with my left hand and jerked it open, only to face a spray of bullets, one of which burned into my gut. I slammed the door closed.

More gunfire sounded from the main stairs where Connor and Marko were.

I gasped in pain as more and more of my nerve endings reported to my brain.

Gut shots hurt! This was a lot worse than a bullet in my shoulder. Or even one in my side.

But, I reminded myself, it wasn't going to kill me, and I didn't have time to wallow in the pain. I had to get to Emma and Mason.

I opened the door again, this time staying behind it. Then, with a handgun in each hand, I ran into the stairwell, shooting before I could even see anything to hit.

Which was fortunate.

The man had been right by the door, rifle raised. He shot me, this time in my right arm — but my bullet spray knocked him back and down four steps. I put two insurance bullets in his head as I stepped over him and ran down the rest of the stairs.

Nobody was behind the door as I exited the stairwell. I sped past open doors on this floor with two or four bunks inside each. Blankets suggested they were in use, but nobody was inside the rooms.

Nobody's sleeping with that alarm blasting our eardrums!

Rounding a corner I saw Marko fastening a big compression bandage around one of Connor's thighs. The front of his snow suit soaked red with blood.

I gasped in horror. Connor saw me and said, "Not the femoral. I'll be okay."

Suddenly I could breathe again. I noticed the two men lying dead behind them.

Danny's voice sounded in my ear. "Still no sign of Mason or Emma. But there was one armed man standing outside a door down the hall to Connor's right who isn't there any longer. I can't see if he went into the room behind him."

I nodded at Connor.

Marko's eyes widened, staring at my stomach. I looked at the hole and the blood oozing out of it. Son-of-a-gun, just seeing it doubled the pain I felt.

I needed to transform soon, in order to heal.

I gritted my teeth and said, "It's nothing. Just a scratch." I tried to sound convincing, but must have failed.

Marko came toward me, pulling out more bandages. "I know a gut wound when I see one. We have to stabilize you."

"I'll be fine. Go rescue Emma and Mason."

He shook his head and kept moving towards me.

I lifted my 1911 and pointed it at him.

"Rescue them *right now*. Do your job!"

His eyes opened in shock. He looked down the gun barrel and his face turned red in anger.

"Okay, you crazy bitch. Whatever you say."

He pulled out another handgun and — both guns now leading the way — turned into the only remaining hallway on the floor, the one to Connor's right. He disappeared.

I leaned heavily back against the wall and used my fists to rub the tears flooding my eyes from the pain.

Connor was staring at me, then started towards me.

I raised my gun again. "Not you, too. Go find Mason."

He raised an eyebrow. "You going to shoot me? I don't think so."

I rolled my eyes. "It's nothing serious."

"Show me."

I couldn't. As soon as I transformed, the red, ragged wound would be gone. Well... the only good defense is offense.

"You're compromising our team's efficiency. Either you trust me or you don't. I've never been a fucking martyr and I'm not about to start now. I'm fine. Go!"

Boy, what a look he gave me. There was so much I couldn't read into it. But he turned and went down the hall after Marko.

I leaned hard against a wall and covered my ears.

I'd kill anybody if it would stop that damn alarm!

I looked down and saw — thankfully — the blood oozing from my stomach had slowed. Almost stopped.

I gritted my teeth. When you know you'll heal, lying around moaning in pain feels... indulgent somehow. The pain was real, very real. But... I think we use blinding pain to warn us we're in risk of dying. So we don't move and we get help. But since I know I'm not going to die, aren't I just being a crybaby?

And how the hell do I get so sidetracked by questions better left for times when people aren't in danger?

I pushed away from the wall and, looking around to make sure nobody else was around, followed the two men around the corner.

I had to finish this fast and get away — or my body was going to transform without my permission.

Then I would really be screwed.

CHAPTER THIRTY-THREE

Mason

Mason looked at the time on his laptop. It was 12:10 AM, ten minutes later than the last time he looked.

When would Sara come? He'd left the message late last night, so logically he could expect her right about now. This was 24-26 hours since he received his friend Steve's message. But that assumed his reply was in code, and that Steve had understood Mason's message and managed to reach Sara with it.

Sara had told him once that one AM was the military's preferred time to launch an attack. She'd found it in the reading she did, and confirmed it with Connor.

Would it be tonight? Tomorrow? Or never? It made his head hurt, and he massaged his temples.

He wasn't supposed to see Emma for another hour, but...

What if they came earlier?

That was it. He wasn't going to lose Emma because he wasn't sure when, or if, Sara would come tonight. He had a lot of regrets in his life, but he wasn't adding that one.

He leaned over the Lenovo and stealthily removed the stylus from the right side of the laptop's casing, then slipped it inside his jeans pocket. It was the only thing he had that could be used as a weapon.

He stood up and walked to the cell door. It was unlocked, but one of Felix's goons was always outside with a gun.

Eddie was his guard tonight, a man who distinguished himself from Joe Bob only by his hair and a stupid-looking mustache and a soul-patch on his chin. Mason had fantasized about using it as a bulls-eye for a bullet. But with only a stylus for a weapon, it wouldn't work — he'd just hit a bunch of teeth.

No, the pen would be better at the neck. He knew there were arteries there, although he didn't know where they were. But he did know where the trachea was.

What else he could do?

He didn't even know if he'd be able to actually attack someone... to kill someone... or more than one someone.

He *did* know he would try.

He nodded at Eddie and said, "I'm waiting on a program to run. If I visit Emma now, I'll be back here by the time the program has some answers."

He'd used the same tactic the day before, when he'd decided to contact Sara. Joe Bob was on the door then and had called Felix to get his approval.

The goons must talk to each other because this one simply nodded his head and said, "Let's go."

They went up a flight of stairs and stopped at the door to Emma's room. Joe Bob was guarding her door, and he opened it for them, then remained outside. Eddie left for wherever he goes when he gets an hour off.

The last time he saw Emma, she was only half awake — the opioid pain killer was messing with her mind. Today her eyes were more alert. More penetrating.

He leaned over to kiss her on the side of her cheek and whispered in her ear. "Do you think you could walk right now?"

Her eyes widened, and she struggled to sit up.

He put a soft hand on her shoulder. "No, no, don't try to get up. He leaned back down and whispered, "It's only a maybe for tonight. Or maybe tomorrow. About this time."

He straightened back up and looked at her. She grinned at him, but it looked stilted. She said, "I dreamed about dancing. Would you like to go dancing one of these days?"

Dancing? "I'd love to," he said, taking her remaining hand in his. Tears pooled in his eyes.

You don't go dancing with "just a friend," do you?

He sat down beside her, holding her remaining hand. "So, where should we go on vacation after this? Is there anyplace you've always wanted to go?"

How could a woman look so sad, even though she was smiling?

"How about Manchu Picchu? she asked. "I always thought..."

Mason watched her face light up as she described a trip they were never likely to make. He let her words transport them both out of this nightmare.

An ear-splitting alarm sounded, making both of them jump.

"Intruder alert," he heard. "Plan Omega... Intruder alert... Plan Omega."

The door to the room opened, and Joe Bob came rushing in, rifle raised towards Emma.

Mason jumped up and put himself between Emma and the gun.

"Move," said Joe Bob.

Mason did move, straight towards the man. "You can't shoot me," he said. "Felix would have your head. He needs me."

"He doesn't need your knees to work. Last chance." He pointed the rifle right at Mason's knee.

"No!" Emma screamed.

The man's head turned towards her, for just a second.

Mason lunged forward, stylus in his hand. He jabbed it into the man's throat as hard as he could.

Mason heard the rifle shoot and felt a blinding pain in his right knee. His attack caused Joe Bob to fall back, and Mason collapsed on top of him.

Mason pulled out the stylus and slammed it again into Joe Bob's throat.

Underneath him, Joe Bob twisted and jerked, trying to dislodge Mason. He was making horrible, gasping noises as he tried to get air to his lungs, past the holes in his trachea.

Mason hit him again and again, puncturing his throat. Blood spurted out of the man's neck and coated Mason, but he wouldn't stop. He couldn't.

Mason jerked when he felt a hand touch his shoulder. He twisted around to see Emma, crouched beside him.

"It's okay," she said. "He's gone. It's okay."

Mason blinked and noticed all the blood. *Oh, no.* His stomach roiled and his lips clamped together.

He would not be sick. No! He tasted vomit in his mouth but swallowed. Emma was talking. He shook his head.

"Your knee!"

Mason looked down and realized he wasn't going to be any help getting Emma out of here.

Emma leaned her head forward, on his shoulder. It felt so right.

"Get his weapon," she said.

"What? Oh... right. Right." Mason pulled the rifle off the guy — the dead guy. *Holy shit!* He scooted back to lean against the wall and nearly passed out from the pain.

He gasped — deep breaths — one after another. He would *not* pass out.

He looked around the room for another weapon. Something that might work like a club? Nothing.

Emma got up and picked up a green something that was shaped like a hardshell briefcase. Mason thought it might be a defibrillator. That might work.

They heard gunshots. A lot of them.

They glanced at each other and stared at the door. He hoped it was Sara... and that they weren't getting shot out there.

Should he go out and help? Crawl if he had to?

No. All he could do right now was protect Emma — and he would. No matter the cost.

"Your people?" she asked him.

Mason inhaled. "I sure hope so."

Emma moved to the other side of the door and prepared to wield her suitcase.

They waited.

Hours went by. Or at least it seemed like that.

A man's head popped into the room, then right back out. Emma swung the briefcase which slammed against the wall where his face had appeared. *So fast!* Mason's finger hadn't started to squeeze trigger before the man was gone.

He heard the man say, "Mason? Emma? We're here to rescue you both."

Mason wasn't feeling real trusting. "Who're you with?" he called back.

"Connor's here with me. And Sara. Can I come in?"

"If you put the gun down. No bad guys left in here."

"Okay. The gun is down." The man's head popped back in the room, then he walked in, still holding a rifle, but pointing it down. He looked around, bent down and stared at the bloody mess of a throat on the dead man. His eyes paused then widened as he saw Emma's missing hand and Mason's knee.

Connor came in the room, followed by Sara. She rushed to kneel beside him. She grabbed his shoulders as though she wanted to shake him, pulled him towards her in a hug, then stopped — looking at his knee. "Oh, Mason!"

She did shake him after that. "If you *ever* let yourself get kidnapped again, I swear I'll kill you myself."

Mason had to grin. "Yeah, I love you too, Sara."

"Arrrggghhh." She crushed him in another hug.

Connor tapped his mic and said, "Danny, any more hostiles?" He listened, then said, "Good."

"Danny," Sara said, tapping hers. "Please please do something about this damn alarm!"

She turned to Marko and said, "You'll have to get Mason up two flights. Can you?"

Marko rolled his eyes at her, and said to Mason, "I'm cutting your pant leg." As he did, Mason swallowed a scream and the bile that rose in his throat. It looked as bad as it felt.

Marko lowered a pack from his back and reached inside. He pulled out some sort of contraption that Mason had never seen before. Marko lifted his leg and put a loose cuff around his knee, then — holding the knee slightly bent — he pressed a button and foam came out, encasing the knee under the cuff.

Mason felt it engulf his knee and then solidify. It was like an instant cast.

"FastCast," Marko said. "You'll be able to walk on it in a minute. It'll hurt, but not like it would otherwise.

Sara had moved over to Emma and was staring at her missing hand. Mason heard the horror in her voice as she asked, "They did this?"

"Yes," Emma said.

Suddenly both Sara and Marko put their hands to their ears.

"What?" she asked. "What did he look like?"

She nodded and turned to Mason. "Was anyone here shorter and skinnier than the big guys we've seen like this one?" She kicked the body lying there.

Mason nodded and said, "Felix. He's running the place. Shorter and thinner than me."

She nodded then talked into a mic. Mason saw it was one he'd designed for her. He smiled, approvingly, then heard her say, "And you're sure he couldn't have gone past you? Or out the other top door?"

"You're both hurt," Mason said, looking at Sara's gut wound and Connor's blood-soaked leg wrapped with a bandage and a funny-looking clip.

Sara paced. "I don't like this. Connor? Marko? Why would the leader cut and run? Unless..."

Connor's face went white. "You think he's like Johnson in Texas? He's wired the place to blow?"

Marko grabbed Mason and moved towards the door, half serving as a cane for him.

Sara yelled, "Everyone — out now!" Then she tapped her mic and said, "Danny, get a couple of snowmobiles up here. You're responsible for Connor and Emma. I'm going after this Felix."

She stopped at Connor. "You can get up the stairs?"

"Yes. Go get him."

Sara dashed past everyone and was gone.

CHAPTER THIRTY-FOUR

Sara

I ran up the back stairway, hitting a railing in my hurry which jarred the hole in my gut that was already starting to heal. I could feel the damn bullet inside being pushed out towards my skin. It hurt!

I felt a grin spread across on my face. *Mason's alive!*

Well... at least right now. If this place doesn't explode in the next few minutes.

I leapt over the dead body on the stairs and ran to the office where the coffee had still been warm.

I leveled both my handguns and shot the outside wall of the office. The one that just might be hiding a way out.

Yes! The bullets pinged against metal behind the wall. I grabbed the desk and slammed it hard around the metal, looking for a door. I grabbed siding on the front and peeled it back, finding the door but looking for a way to open it.

I heard footsteps running up the center stairs and yelled out, "Over here — it's a quicker way out."

Finally, I found the latch. There had undoubtedly been some secret lever in the office that opened it, but brute force worked too. I pushed on the latch and the door swung open, leading into a tunnel that expanded and had another door at the far end. Two snowmobiles were waiting there, beside an empty spot designed for a third.

Marko entered the room. He nodded at me and turned back to help the others.

I hit buttons by the outside door, and as it slid open, tapped my mic, saying, "Danny?"

"Almost to the snowmobiles," he said.

"We found the exit Felix used to escape. Everyone's here and there are two extra vehicles. I'm taking one in pursuit. Get everyone else out of here as fast as you can."

"Got it."

I dug into my snowsuit and pulled out my hat, face mask and gloves — shoving them on as quickly as I could, listening for the sounds of a loud snowmobile. I needed to know which way Felix had gone. Thankfully these escape vehicles were not electric or I'd have no chance of hearing him. It had been, what? Four minutes since he'd left? Five?

And then I heard it, a faint motor, but it was the only other sound in the vast snowy wilderness. It was amplified a little as it echoed through mountains.

I jerked one of the snowmobiles through the door, hit the starter button, and started down the hill as fast as I could.

Could I catch him? Assuming the sleds were all equal — the two that had remained were identical — the only difference would be body weight. Too bad the guy wasn't twice my weight like Marko. Mason had said Felix was smaller and thinner than him. I'd never weighed Mason, but guessed he was around 160 pounds, so Felix could be 145-150? That was only 15-20 more than me.

I shook my head. I might not be able to catch Felix.

I gasped when I heard a single rifle shot behind me. Should I turn around? No. There were three men back there who were able to handle it.

But... what if they shot Mason? Or Connor?

If so, going back there wouldn't change whatever happened. I reminded myself of what had always been so hard for me to learn: trust your team. You're not alone anymore... you have good people around you... trust them.

Well... I was *trying to.*

I may still have gone back, but then the transformation started. When I'm badly hurt, my body will change to my other form, whether or not I want it to. I can put it off a little while, with some effort, but sooner or later....

My body jerked in agony, my hands flew off the handlebars and I fell to the snow unzipping my snowsuit as fast as I could.

I unclipped the strap holding my faux-fur hat just as my fingers turned to claws.

My feet shrunk into paws and fell out of my snow boots. I squeezed my eyes tightly and held my breath as fur covered my skin in the warmest of layers. When the pain finally stopped, I wanted to lie there, oh... for an hour or two.

But Felix was getting away.

I could chase him as a wolf, but my top speed was 37 miles per hour and I couldn't hold it long. Gas powered snowmobiles can run at 100 MPH for as long as they have fuel.

I stuck my snout into the snowsuit's inside pockets and pulled out two of the four sealed packets of salmon. Using a paw to hold each down, I used my teeth to rip off the tops and — literally — wolf down the contents.

I scrunched my eyes closed as I waited for the pain to hit.

Nothing.

What the hell?

I'd wanted to save the other two salmon packets in case I had to do this again, but...

I couldn't let Felix get away. Hopefully two more would do the trick?

I quickly ate both of them. I'd better not require more — because I was out!

I think I lost several years of my life when, again, nothing happened. At first.

Finally. Finally! I felt the change start. Slowly, almost begrudgingly. I was deliriously happy to feel the pain.

A minute later, I was re-fastening my human clothes. The snowmobile had stopped when my hands flew off the handlebars, so I jumped back on it.

Then I listened.

Without the sound of my snowmobile, I could hear his better.

Damn! It sounded at least two miles away. Without my improved hearing, I'd be lost here.

I started the engine and took off again in the direction in Felix's direction. With my engine running, I lost his sound. But... Felix had been traveling the same trajectory from the start.

I decided to ride straight ahead and stop every 20 minutes or so to make sure he hadn't turned.

As I chased him, I tried to add up the number of transformations I'd done recently. There were four last night as I shadowed Connor and two more right now. In addition, I had to heal myself from a gut shot as well as a bullet to my shoulder.

I'd never pushed myself like this before. Maybe I was hitting a limit on how often I could do it?

I sighed and mentally crossed my fingers that there was no limit.

My actual fingers squeezed as hard as they could to make this sled run faster.

CHAPTER THIRTY-FIVE

Connor

Connor watched Sara speed off after the asshole who'd been running this mess.

If there was a bomb, they had to leave now. As Emma and Mason were squeezing onto the back of a snowmobile, he flung open doors of a nearby cabinet. Inside it he found water and food, but they had those waiting at their own rides. He grabbed a handful of blankets and tossed them at Mason. "Wrap yourselves up in these."

He turned to Marko, who told him, "Come back for me," and then launched himself out the door — first running to the deep snow, then belly flopping and sliding down the hill as fast as he could go.

Seeing Mason & Emma wrapped and ready, Connor jumped on the front of the snowmobile and took off, heading for where they'd left the electric sleds.

Halfway down the hill, he saw Danny riding towards them. Connor yelled at him to go get Marko, then continued on to the remaining three sleds. They were parked as far under an overhang as possible.

Connor ran to his parked sled and grabbed the extra backpack he'd brought with clothes for Mason and Emma. He threw them at the two, saying, "Get dressed as fast as you can."

He turned and watched as Danny rode towards them with Marko behind him.

Inexplicably, the two men went flying up into the air, as if they'd been launched by a catapult. They were coming right at him. Except... Connor realized he was also flying. And spinning.

A low, hollow-sounding boom rang through the air, a boom of thunder so deep and long he wondered how close the lightening was. Except, there was no lightening.

He landed on his side, a bolt of pain reminding him of the bullet still in his leg. He turned to look back up the mountain they'd just left and saw a geyser of smoke.

Son-of-a-bitch. It really was *set to explode.*

He heard a second explosion. This time flames shot into the air, along with pieces of flying metal.

"Their diesel tank," someone said beside him, and Connor turned to find Danny standing there. He looked around. Everyone was safe. They were all standing in shock and staring at where they'd just been.

"Anyone hurt?" he asked and was relieved to see heads shaking no.

Connor swallowed, then tapped his mic. "Sara, can you hear me?"

He heard only static.

"Sara? Please answer."

Nothing.

Danny looked at Connor. "We have to drive to our other snowmobiles — these electrics can't get us far enough on the batteries we brought. And we won't all fit on the two gas models."

"Do that. Mason and Emma need doctors. Get Judy on it. I'm going after Sara."

Mason put a hand on his arm. "No."

"No? You don't want me to help Sara?"

Mason laughed, but it sounded forced. "Don't be funny. Felix is just one skinny man. Sara would not appreciate you chasing after her, implying she couldn't handle him."

Connor shook his head.

Mason squeezed his arm. "Trust me, Connor. She'd be furious. And you need a doctor too."

Connor scowled. "You and I are going to talk. Soon."

"Sure." Mason looked away.

Connor could see "talking" was the last thing Mason wanted to do. Well... too damn bad.

Connor looked around. They had his gas-powered sled and the four electrics they came with, but Emma wasn't operating one without a left hand, and he didn't think Mason's knee could take the jerks and slams of driving, even with his temporary cast.

He put Emma behind Marko and Mason behind Danny, making the weights nearly equal. He divided up the extra batteries from the two sleds they were leaving behind. He took the largest duffle bag loaded with their heaviest equipment for his own sled.

Danny and Marko started off. Connor was about to follow them when he paused, thinking he heard something he wasn't expecting.

A helicopter.

Yes, a long shadow was moving over his overhang, moving towards the two men and their passengers.

He tapped his mic and yelled, "Chopper. Try to find cover."

Only there really wasn't any.

The overhang that he was under was the only shelter in sight and it barely covered half his sled.

He grabbed the bag of their biggest weapons and unzipped it.

Marko and Danny veered off in separate directions, Marko headed back towards him.

Connor unzipped the bag and grabbed one of the Matador rocket launchers that Marko had brought. He'd raised an eyebrow at the time, but finally agreed because they might need to demolish the facility afterwards.

Good thinking, Marko!

Rifle shots came from the helicopter.

Connor's fingers fumbled for a warhead, rejecting the rounded, plastic tips of the two HESH models. Instead, he grabbed one of the pointed-end HEAT warheads designed to penetrate metal.

He saw a flash from the helicopter, then Danny's head exploded, and his sled jerked to one side, turning over.

Damnit!

Connor slammed the HEAT warhead into the Matador.

Mason had fallen from the back of Danny's sled and was rolling when a flash of gray came from nowhere and covered him.

A wolf?

Bullets strafed the snow, hitting Danny again and leaving a path of red stains where Mason lay.

Connor lifted the Matador to his shoulder and aimed for the helicopter.

Was the damn helicopter armored? If so, he'd be lucky to stop it. It wasn't an Apache or a Black Hawk, but he wasn't up on new military models.

Marko had stopped and rolled his sled, sheltering underneath it. He'd tucked his vulnerable head and was using his body armor to cover Emma.

The helicopter continued firing, crossing the snow and moving towards Marko's sled, when...

Finally! Finally!

The helicopter was only 150 feet from him when Connor could finally fire. The missile was barely off before Connor dropped the Matador and reached for a second one.

From the corner of his eye, he saw the chopper rise suddenly and veer away from him, then point nose down and head straight for the ground.

It burst into flames as it hit.

Connor sped towards Danny and Mason, although he knew from what he'd seen that Danny was never getting up ever again.

He stopped by the wolf covering Mason. He was almost afraid to look. They had rescued Mason. He'd been safe. He could *not* be dead now.

He knelt and touched the wolf, who was certainly dead. Three bullet holes, each leaking blood, stitched the length of its body. Marko ran up beside him, Emma following as fast as she could move in boots that were too big — her feet were slipping around in them.

"Mason!" Emma screamed as she ran, stumbled, fell, and scrambled back up.

Connor moved to pick up the wolf but stopped when it rose up itself, as Mason lifted it and scurried out from underneath. He was covered in blood.

Emma fell on her knees in front of him and cried, "Where are you hurt?"

"My shoulder."

Connor looked and saw in and out bullet holes in the ski jacket. The rest of the blood must be from the wolf.

Mason turned to the wolf. A look of horror flashed across his face as he saw the bullet holes and blood.

"Sa..." Mason clamped his lips shut and turned the wolf over, appearing shocked as he stared at its penis.

Connor frowned at Mason. *What the hell?*

He told Mason, "Sara had some wolves help in the attack. They drew out three men before we went in."

Mason stared at him. "Wolves don't... they wouldn't...." He went silent.

Marko had disappeared, then came back with bandages. He bared Mason's shoulder, worked on it, then zipped him back up.

"We need to get out of here now," Marko said.

Connor agreed. "I'll carry Danny and the gear bags on the diesel. You take Mason and Emma."

Marko asked, "Do we take the wolf?"

Mason looked at the wolf and said, "Call Sara."

Connor frowned and tapped his mic. This time she answered.

He explained how one of the wolves saved Mason's life and died in the process. "Mason said to ask you what we should do about him."

Sara said in his ear, "Is it the gray wolf or one of the white ones?"

"Gray."

"Put him under the overhang and cover him with any extra clothing or blankets you have... and, Connor? You listening?"

"I'm here."

"I hid a bag. It's over where you saw the wolves first surround me. Get it and put it near the wolf."

Cover him? Connor stared at Mason, but he told Marko to do it, then said into his mic, "Why?"

The silence went on so long that he thought Sara was gone. Then she said, "The other wolves will come back for him. What's in the bag is for them. Please don't look in it."

Marko placed Sara's bag with the dead wolf, under the overhang. He threw blankets, and every article of clothing they didn't need, on top of the wolf and weighted it down with an overturned sled.

Then they packed up quickly and left.

Connor promised himself very, very long talks with both Mason and Sara.

CHAPTER THIRTY-SIX

Sara

I chased Felix across snow-covered mountains and evergreen-clogged valleys. It was dark, but the moon and a billion stars lit the night even to my poor eyesight. It was beautiful, but hard to enjoy after Connor's message.

Danny was dead. While on a job for me. There wasn't enough alcohol in the world to make that guilt go away.

But... I couldn't think about it now. My right hand squeezed so hard on the gas that I was surprised I didn't crush the handlebar. Going that fast, I had little warning about bumps in the path until I was flying up and slamming back down with spine-jarring effect.

I was grateful my gut had healed, or I would have been screaming in pain.

Mason was shot again — so glad I didn't see that.

Running Wolf saved Mason's life. I owed the old man big time. I hoped the food in my bag and the clothes would keep him safe until he could transform back into wolf and leave with his pack.

The fuel gauge told me we had to be close to Felix's destination.

Unless he was just driving into the middle of nowhere. Maybe to get picked up on some mountain top?

I frowned. I thought I heard something — barely — over the roar of the engine.

I glanced up and nearly had a heart attack. I saw lights moving in the sky. A black-painted helicopter was flying about a mile ahead of me.

Then it pointed straight down.

Shit!

I jerked the sled to hide in a nearby group of trees and turned it off. Due to the helicopter noise, they probably hadn't heard me.

There was no tree cover ahead I could use to get near to where the helicopter was landing. It was dark, but not dark enough to hide in, with the half moon and all the stars.

My white snowsuit would stand out like a beacon, unless I crawled in it. And I didn't have enough time. If they were picking Felix up, they'd be gone before I could get close to them.

I had to go in as a wolf.

But... could I? Would my body transform yet again?

When an injury wasn't forcing my transformation, I could simply will my body to turn from human to wolf. The return — from wolf to human — was harder and required I eat protein.

But... even if I could turn to wolf, I'd eaten all my protein sources. How would I turn back?

Stop it! While you overthink everything, Felix could get away.

I took off my clothes and stashed them in the rear compartment. *Positive thinking here, Sara. You* will *be able to do this!*

Then I mentally reached for my wolf form.

And reached.

And... there was just a glimmer of fur I could see in my mind, just a glimpse. I focused on it. Pulled it closer.

And... the change came.

The relief was so great, I barely felt the pain. Then I ran on all fours, as fast as I could, towards where the chopper had landed.

Two minutes later, I came up behind it. It was a boxy model with seats for six men plus two pilots. It had a long tail and I saw two numbers written on it — a four and an eight. Other numbers were there, but they were obscured by what looked like mud. Except there wasn't any mud around here.

There was no name or other identifier on it — just those numbers.

I moved to the tail, stood on my hind legs and rubbed a paw along the row of numbers. The "mud" was a tar-like brown substance which stuck to my fur.

But I got the full inscription: 80428.

About 500 feet past the helicopter, I saw a small white dome that was built into the side of a hill, now revealing an open door. Four giant men in combat gear surrounded it, as a small guy in an eye-blinding, lime-green snowsuit came out.

Despite looking like a child among men, he was full of himself. Cocky. Maybe it was *because* of who he had surrounding and protecting him.

Chopping off Emma's hand didn't take courage. It just took evil.

I wanted to squeeze the life out of his throat, so I tried — hard — to think of some way to stop him. But taking on four armed mercenaries would be suicide with no firepower.

I dropped down and trotted away from the helicopter, moving in a straight line that kept as much of the tail blocking their view of me as possible.

Behind me, I heard the engine rev as it took to the air. I looked up as it flew over me. Too late I saw a man lean out the door and point a rifle at me.

I sped up and felt a searing pain in my ear before I heard the shot. I went down, rolled over, and was back up running fast.

I heard laughter as the chopper then passed over me and was gone.

I spent a moment cursing this damn state of Alaska, with every terrible word I'd ever heard. I expected some men to be evil. But what the hell kind of government thinks it's just dandy to kill living, thinking, feeling creatures for fun and giggles?

I pictured myself ripping the throat out of the asshole responsible. Except that was the governor and most of the 60 members of the legislature. Too many. And they'd only be replaced with similar-thinking assholes.

I sat in the snow and ran a paw over my head. It came away bloody.

I frowned, then swept the top of my paw back over my right ear and discovered I was missing a serious chunk of myself.

It stung like a yellowjacket, but it wasn't enough to force a change. Fortunately. Because I had no interest in walking a mile and a half, naked, back to my snowmobile in what had to be minus ten degrees.

I turned back to the dome and went to investigate. There was no lever or knob on the door. Instead, a keypad was embedded into the side, requiring a combination I didn't have.

I shoved on the door, but it didn't miraculously open.

Well, at least I had the helicopter tail number.

I rubbed my paw over my torn ear again and this time there was no blood. I found a clean patch of loose snow and rubbed my head in it, the snow numbing the sting.

I was already healing. I *loved* being a werewolf!

It was a slower trip as I trotted back to my snowmobile. I considered my options. The snowmobile had enough gas to only make it half way back to the bunker, which was not enough of a reason to change back into human form.

But, if I stayed a wolf, I could only go to my cabin, which was that direction, but miles past the bunker. Maybe I'd run into Running Wolf and could traverse home with his pack.

Unfortunately, it would take two days. That was a problem for two reasons. I wanted to get Steve — or hopefully Mason! — on the helicopter tail number as quickly as possible. Also, I didn't know what my team would do if I disappeared for that long without notice.

A funny idea crossed my mind.

No... that would be too crazy.

And it probably wouldn't work.

I snorted, then realized my tongue was hanging far out in a wolf grin. Hell, it might be fun to at least try it.

Although I would be so screwed if anyone happened to see me.

I got back to the sled and stared at it. At least it was upright. I pushed to make sure the cargo box latch was closed. I didn't want my human clothes falling out.

Then I jumped up on the snowmobile seat. I didn't need to worry about working the brakes. But could I work the throttle? My right hand had to squeeze it to make the thing go. The harder the squeeze, the faster it would move.

My paw wasn't squeezing anything.

I thought I could sit with my haunches on the seat, then lean my body hard against the handlebars, my paw pushing the throttle in.

I tried it and jerked forward. *Aha!*

Then my paw slipped off the throttle, the sled died, and I went flying off into the snow.

I tried again, this time with my back legs straddling the seat. Again my paw slipped and I flew off.

Determined now, I lay myself out on the seat, all four legs spread out to the sides. I could even squeeze my four legs in slightly to get a grip on the seat, although a weak one.

I stretched my neck out to the right and took the handlebar and throttle in my mouth and bit down. Gently.

The snowmobile moved forward. Slowly.

I bit harder and the sled moved faster... and faster.

The sled lifted a little in the air as we crested a bump and the jolt when it hit the ground rattled my lower teeth. My uppers were happy with the rubber handlebar, but the metal-only throttle on my lower teeth was a problem.

If I cracked a tooth, would it heal the next time I transformed? Probably.

Hmm.

Better question — could I order myself a custom snowmobile with a rubber-wrapped throttle?

Because this was kind of fun.

Lying flat out, I sped through the snow as if I were a bird. It was at least three times faster than I could run on all fours. I was soaring!

You go fast in human form too, but you're completely encased in snowsuit, helmet, facemask, etc. It doesn't feel anything like what I was feeling now.

The wind was ruffling through my fur, even flattening it, caressing it along my body.

I wanted to laugh and scream in joy,.

Until I hit a bump and chipped at least two molars. *Ow!*

Ignoring the pain, I gripped my jaws harder on the controls and continued riding until my fuel ran out with about three more miles left to go to the bunker where Mason had been held. And another 15 past that to my cabin.

I planned to take a wide circle around the bunker — or what remained of it — just in case the owners sent more people there.

I had to do the rest of the way on paws.

The problem with traveling as a wolf was that I had no pockets to hold anything. That was why I'd had a special backpack made with straps that I could slip into while in wolf form. I'd brought it to this battle, then had asked Connor leave it by Running Wolf's body. It was in case he needed the clothes or the food inside, once he'd transformed and healed.

It was also great for carrying coms equipment. My only other choice would be in my mouth, but I suspected my saliva would be disastrous for the electronics.

I decided as close as I was — probably three miles — it was worth going to see if Running Wolf had left my backpack. He might have just eaten the food and left with his wolf pack. The custom bag could be laying right there, ready for me.

But... if he took the clothes, I didn't want to come three miles back here for the ones in my snowmobile.

I used a claw to open the back compartment and pulled my snow-suit out, taking care not to puncture it with my teeth. I checked to make sure the coms were in the pockets, as were the hat and face mask.

I looked longingly at the boots, but that wasn't happening.

Groaning at the awkwardness of it, I stuck a fang through the eyelet of the zipper and started off — dragging the suit beside me. It kept getting under me and tripping me. This was going to be the longest three miles I'd ever gone.

I was about halfway there when two wolves appeared. Then two more. I could recognize each one by smell; they were in Running Wolf's pack.

Why were they still here?

They moved towards where I assumed he'd been shot, looking back at me. They wanted me to follow.

Curious, and now worried, I did.

An hour later, as I climbed a rise, I saw three more wolves in the distance. I also saw a smashed and blackened helicopter lying in the snow.

Two of the new wolves were lying on the snow. Only... not really. They were lying on something as white as the snow — but it looked like human skin.

One of them rose, and I could see the white thing on the ground was Running Wolf, human and naked. He looked dead.

Except, how could that be?

I rushed to him and lay my head on his chest. He was a solid block of ice. There was no pulse, no heartbeat, no breathing.

Could he come back from this? Could I de-thaw him and revive him?

I didn't think so. No matter how badly I'd been injured, my heart still beat. My lungs still breathed.

This wasn't a damned vampire movie, where a dead creature reanimates. Regardless of form, werewolves are alive. More alive — in my opinion — than mere humans.

But... what I saw before me shouldn't be.

He was shot. So what? He would have transformed to human and been healed. I quickly searched his body and saw I was right. There were no bullet holes in him. All he'd had to do was transform back into wolf. Or put on the clothes if he wanted to stay human.

And... there was my backpack. Right beside him. It had been opened and the food packets and clothes were neatly spread out. He'd awakened as a human and did this.

Then he purposefully did not eat the food or put on the warm clothes.

His choice. But why...?

Tears flooded my eyes.

He was kin, in a way, and I'd never got to know him.

I could have learned Hand Talk, like Judy did. He had a world of knowledge, forever closed off to me now.

I didn't understand.

I sat back in the snow and sighed. The wolves came and rubbed up against me.

My god, what must they be feeling? This wolf was there for them all their lives, and for their pack for multiple generations. He must have seemed to be the wisest of elders to them. And strong — so dominant that none of them could have challenged him. Those who wanted to lead a pack of their own would have had to leave this one.

Who would lead them now?

My snowsuit squawked and I looked at it.

A voice came over my coms. "Sara, are you there? It's Marko. I've got a helicopter in case you need pickup."

Quickly, I grabbed the food packets laid out by Running Wolf and shoved them into my snowsuit. I dragged it as fast as I could the 150 yards to the overhang we'd first parked our snowmobiles under. I ripped open all six food packets and wolfed down the protein. Maybe more fuel would mean a more likely transition — even when my body was over extended.

I lay down and crossed claws on both front paws. *Please! Please!*

I sighed as I felt the change come.

Damnit! Transformation to human complete, I gasped for air.

Reminder to self: no sighing at the start of a transformation. Leave a little air in your lungs for the 45 seconds you can't breathe while transforming.

I grabbed the coms unit and said, "Marko? Good. Pick me up at the overhang where we launched our attack."

Then I dressed as quickly as possible. I was very grateful I'd put a pair of snow boots in the pack I'd left for Running Wolf.

"We've got a body to take back," I told Marko as he stepped out of the helicopter. "It's the guy that trained this wolf pack. I don't understand how he got here, or why he removed his clothes, but he's dead."

Marko nodded and together we carried Running Wolf's body to the helicopter and strapped him down. Marko sat beside him.

The pilot turned back to us and said, "We good to go?"

I ran back out and grabbed my custom backpack. When I turned to get back in the chopper, the wolves, who had disappeared when the helicopter landed, reappeared.

"Give me a second," I told the pilot. Then I walked towards the wolves and shook my head at them, at a loss for what to do. They'd lost the only alpha they'd ever known.

One of the wolves — a female — came forward. After a second, a male joined her. Good. I nodded. I could smell they were the parents of all but two of the wolves. They were assuming responsibility.

I laid my forehead against each of theirs.

Then I turned and got in the helicopter, leaving them to make their own way back home.

On the trip back, I asked Marko about Mason and Emma.

"They're on a charter to Tulsa. Your gal Judy was smart to get them into the same hospital because they were not going to be separated."

"Connor?"

"He went with them."

Marko took a breath. "Okay. Mission's over. How're you so strong in arm wrestling?"

Thank god for Google search. It had taken me just two minutes to find a plausible answer for this expected question. "EMS - Electrical MyoStimulation. I've used it on my right arm since I was 10 years old and needed a way to shut up a local bully."

"It won't increase strength that much."

"Twice a day for 25 years? Oh it'll do it. I was just thankful you didn't want to armwrestle left arms."

"But why put all that time into it?"

"I grew up in a rough neighborhood. It kept me out of a lot of fights that I would have lost."

"Huh."

Whew! I think he bought it. Maybe I can use it on Connor too?

I exhaled and changed the subject. "Why'd you come back with a helicopter? That wasn't the plan."

"Mason wouldn't get on the plane unless I agreed to try and find you. He insisted I hover and keep broadcasting for you until I only had enough fuel to get back. It made no sense... first he wouldn't let Connor go after you, then he wanted me to come back now."

I smiled and my vision blurred.

"You'd better not cry. I can't stand broads who cry."

I rubbed my eyes and said, "Trying not to cry is stupid."

I love Mason. He'd been shot up, had a girlfriend missing a hand, and yet he took time to worry about me.

I shook my head. "Mason's like a kid brother to me, but sometimes he acts like he's my father."

CHAPTER THIRTY-SEVEN

Sara

I called Judy from the helicopter and she demanded we bring Running Wolf's body to her at the cabin. She said she'd contact his tribe and get their wishes.

I half-heartedly pushed back on bringing him there, but she calmly said I brought him there now or she would never talk to me or work for me again.

Then she hung up.

I put the phone away and twisted my mouth into a smile. That answered a question running around in my mind — whether she and Running Wolf had become more than acquaintances.

Then I worried. Judy loved men and she almost always had one around, but I'd never seen her care enough to get upset about one. Until now. She was as upset as I'd ever heard her.

When we landed, Judy met us in full snow gear, with blankets for wrapping Running Wolf's body. Her eyes locked on him and she wouldn't look away. Or talk.

I said I'd go in the cabin to make some calls. I don't think she even heard me.

She laid a blanket out, and Marko helped her lay Running Wolf on it. Then he left with the pilot.

Judy sat beside Running Wolf's body. In the cold. When I couldn't watch any more, I went inside and closed the door.

A loud hiss greeted me. Judy's cat Lola bared her teeth, then ran and hid under the bed.

I needed to call Steve Callahan to get him on the number I'd captured from the helicopter that rescued Felix — but I hesitated.

Steve was good and we'd never have found Mason without him, but... that helicopter was tied to the man running all of this. I needed the best hacker around — someone much better than Felix — so Steve didn't end up dead. Like Danny.

I needed Mason.

My phone vibrated and I looked at it. Somehow I wasn't surprised to see that Mason was texting me:

> I got maybe an hour before I go under the knife, so did you find who's paying Felix?

I smiled and replied:

> Helicopter tail #80428 picked him up. It's likely owned by Neville Huber. Can you track? Max caution.

> On it. Leave Felix to me.

I thought about that. I didn't want Mason to be involved in the messy part of the business. I'd tried to shield him, as the younger brother I considered him to be. But it hadn't worked, and Mason was a man. He had the right to make his own decisions.

> OK. You find me the current location of Neville Huber. He's mine.

The door opened and Judy walked in. She sank down on the bed and appeared to be a thousand miles away.

Lola peeked out from underneath it and rubbed against Judy's legs. Absently, Judy patted her head and patted the bed for the cat to jump up.

Instead Lola looked at me and hissed again.

Judy's eyes focused suddenly on the cat. Then she turned and stared at me. For a very long time.

She pointed a finger towards me and said, "You and I are going to talk. But not now."

I sat there, not knowing what to say. I'd been dreading this.

Judy's eyes went unfocused again and she just sat there. Looking at nothing in the room.

Finally she said, "I sent a plane to pick up Jordan. He's the closest thing Running Wolf's people — the Atkira — have to a leader. He's coming here to claim the body and return it for burial. I have a helicopter waiting for him in Anchorage."

Of course she did. Even in pain the woman kept things running smoothly.

She said, "I can call another helicopter in case you don't want to be here when Jordan gets here.

"Why wouldn't I?"

She looked at me. "Bill's coming with him."

"Call the helicopter," I said, grit in my voice.

Did I want to be here when the man I loved... the man who supposedly loved me... the man who was marrying another woman so he could make pure-bred little baby boys to take his place one day as priest to his tribe....

Did I want to be here when that man came here? Hell no.

Judy placed the call, and we sat there, each scrolling through our phones, saying nothing for the next hour.

Finally my helicopter arrived and I escaped.

In Anchorage, I caught a commercial plane and flew to Tulsa to check on Mason and Connor at the hospital.

CHAPTER THIRTY-EIGHT

Sara

The next day I was sitting in my two-person leather recliner in my home, just outside of Lupiti, Oklahoma. Skidi was lying by my side, rolled onto her back to let me scratch her tummy.

I tried to get some work done, but gave up. My mind was too distracted. Danny's funeral was today, and Connor had told me that I was not to attend.

That didn't sit well with me, but Connor insisted. He said the only thing worse for a woman with kids whose husband is in the military, is for that same man to take high-risk mercenary jobs after he's discharged. Connor said a mercenary's employer needs to be a business, not a person. If it's a person, it's so easy for a widow to focus her anger on that person instead of on her husband for taking the job.

All I could do was authorize the money so Danny's family could recover without any financial worries. Connor promised to take care of that, including a fund for college for his two kids.

Still, it felt wrong, like I was throwing money at something to ease my guilt. Hell, I was doing *exactly* that.

Connor told me, "Danny was living the live he chose. Some of us come out of special ops, and nothing else will ever satisfy us. We need the danger, the intensity, the missions. Otherwise, we'd just drink ourselves to death."

It was the most personal conversation I'd ever had with Connor. "You feel that way too? I asked.

He was quiet for a minute, then said, "You never feel more alive than when you choose to put your life on the line."

I had to shut up, because I felt that way myself. Yes, the company I'd set up helped people who couldn't help themselves. We saved lives. But... the thrill I get when it's me vs. a bad guy.... I love how the world slows down... how I see everything so clearly... how my heartbeat climbs and my body takes in more oxygen... I seem so... Connor had the right word. I seem so much more *alive*.

My secure phone rang with Mason's obnoxious ring tone — the Police's "Every Breath You Take." Every so often I try to wipe that song from my phone. It works for half a day, maybe a day, then, somehow, Mason has it going again.

It's only one of Mason's many irritating pranks, but I took a moment to give thanks that he was still around to annoy me.

"You better not have anything to do with this," Mason immediately said.

"Why hello Sara," I said. "How are you doing? I just wanted to thank you again for saving my ass."

"Yeah, yeah. Pull up the local news on NewsMiner.com"

I grabbed my laptop and typed in the address of the Fairbanks newspaper. When I switched to the local tab, I read that Felix had been reported missing by his sister, who was offering a reward for any news of his whereabouts.

I said, "That wasn't me. You told me to leave him to you."

"I already checked with Connor, and it wasn't him."

"Wow."

"Yeah," Mason said. "Wow. Guess Neville Huber isn't just lethal to outsiders."

I shook my head. "Felix looked so cocky when he got in that helicopter. You'd think he'd better understand the guy he was working for and what he was capable of."

"Gotta go. Emma just woke up."

I listened to the dial tone for a few seconds, smiling. "Emma just woke up" indeed. I was glad that Huber had taken care of Felix. Now Mason could spend his time on happier things — like Emma waking up.

CHAPTER THIRTY-NINE

Sara
1 Week Later

Running Wolf would have been uncomfortable with the size of his funeral. More than 150 people came by to pay their respects at the small cemetery on the outskirts of the tiny town of Lupiti. Here the gravestones were small and simple, but well tended, with single flowers or stones as heartfelt reminders.

He was buried under his real name, but everyone was told that he was the great grandson many times over of the Running Wolf that had been the tribe's shaman in the mid-1800s. Instead of the man himself.

I stood a little back from the mourners. I was there to show my respects too, and to thank him for protecting Mason. But I knew so little about him.

As they lowered his body into the ground, Judy came and stood beside me. I knew she'd been around for the past week, talking with Jordan and Bill.

"Did you ever get an idea as to why?" I asked her. "Why didn't he put on the clothes I'd left for him?"

"Or his wolf fur?" she asked, staring at me.

I winced. "Or that."

I asked the question that had been bothering me this whole time. "Did he want to die?"

Judy turned away from me and stared at the hole in the ground that would be Running Wolf's final resting place.

Softly, almost as though she was talking to herself, she said, "I think he wanted to die over 100 years ago. He felt guilty about his people — that he couldn't protect them. I think he went to Alaska to die, but somehow it never happened. He found peace there, living as a wolf. Living in the now — with no past or future. No thinking."

"And then we came along," I said.

"And then we came," she agreed.

I watched people filling up Running Wolf's grave, throwing dirt on top of him, sealing him in. It felt like shards of glass in my heart.

She said, "When he learned you were attacking that bunker, he saw a way to make his death matter. He wasn't planning to come back."

I sighed. "I wish I could thank him for saving Mason."

"He was happy to."

We both stood there, quiet, for awhile. Finally, she said, "I don't blame you."

I turned to look at her, but she was still looking at the grave.

"For not telling me about you — what you are. I don't blame you. I wouldn't have in your position."

I didn't know what to say.

"Who else knows?"

I took a deep breath. "Just Mason. And Bill."

She nodded.

"What will you do now?" I asked her, trying to change the subject.

She stood there, silent. When I was sure she wouldn't answer, she said, "Do you know, I've never really been alone. Without a man, I mean. My whole life."

I stared at her.

She said, "I think it's time I found out what that would be like." She turned to me and put a hand on my arm.

"Don't call me until we get a new case. And when we do get one, you call me or else."

"I couldn't do one without you," I said, honestly.

She started to walk away, back to where the cars were parked. Then she came back.

"You should probably talk to Bill soon."

I started to object, but she shook her head. "He's not married and he's not getting married. She told him 'no'."

She turned and walked away.

"Wait. What?"

But Judy kept going.

I looked back at the gravesite. People were leaving. My eyes found Bill, who was walking a very pregnant woman back towards the parked cars.

I must have misunderstood Judy.

Then the woman turned. She was very beautiful, with shiny black hair down to her waist, and a regal posture.

She looked across the new grave, right at me.

We stared at each other, then her lips twisted into a sort of smile. She nodded her head, then looked back at Bill and walked with him to his truck. He helped her into the passenger side, then turned to move to the driver's side. His eyes caught mine and he froze.

He looked like a deer in the headlights.

Maybe I did too.

What the hell?

Then he got in, and they drove off.

CHAPTER FORTY

Sara

I was sitting in my Tulsa office twiddling my thumbs when Connor called.

"I'm taking Emma and Mason out of the hospital," he said. "It's not safe."

"What happened?"

"There have been two incidents in the last 14 hours. My night guy raised the alarm about a suspicious orderly. Turns out it wasn't someone who worked for the hospital. Then at eight this morning, my day guy saw a man with flowers walking towards Emma's room. When they locked eyes, he walked into a nearby room. My guy called hospital security and they found the flowers dumped on an empty bed. The man had vanished."

It seemed Neville Huber wasn't satisfied killing Felix. He was determined to kill Emma and surely Mason as well.

I've told my team over and over again that we're in the rescue business, not the killing business. That's why I had asked Mason and Steve to gather all the info we could find on Huber and get it to a federal prosecutor. So we can let the prosecutor take him down.

Mind you, I no longer trust all prosecutors. Rather, I no longer trust the bosses that sign their paychecks. It pains me to say this, but politics and corruption have a foothold in the U.S. justice system. Whether or not someone gets prosecuted can depend on what that person can do for the political party in power.

Huber has a fortune in the billions, not to mention an army of mercenaries, enough to bribe or threaten anyone — even the president, who he undoubtedly knows on a first-name basis.

So I didn't really expect the U.S. to put Huber in jail. I hoped for it and I wanted to give the justice system a chance. And I *really* didn't want my little company to be in the assassination business.

Connor was still talking. "We're moving Mason and Emma onto Lupiti tribal lands. I hired George Chapman, a Lupiti who works as a bodyguard for my old firm, to set up a team to protect them. He's going to hire every household within three blocks of where Mason and Emma will be staying to act as spotters. Any outsider will be reported immediately."

I smiled, picturing it.

"Wait, what about Judy?" I asked. "Could she be at risk? And you?"

"Or you," Connor said, adding, "I'm going to call her next."

I put my cowboy boots up on the desk and finished the bad-for-me Diet Coke I'd opened about half an hour ago. It made me grimace. I'm dumb enough to love the way it burns, going down my throat, but I want it ice-cold. Mine was flat and lukewarm.

Yuck!

What was I going to do about Huber?

My phone rang again, and it was Connor.

"That was quick," I said, surprised.

"Get our lawyer down to cop central for Judy as quickly as you can. She's okay, but the guy who picked up her Mini-Cooper to service it is dead."

"Dead?"

"The car exploded when he started it."

I felt icy fingers close around my heart, make a fist and squeeze.

Judy was still alive but only by chance.

Connor was still talking, when I tuned back in. He said, "I've got another bodyguard meeting me, but he's the last one I know and trust. We've run out of options. Anyone else, Huber could have gotten to."

"You be careful then."

"You too. If you're in your office, get out. You're a sitting duck there."

"Will do." I stood up, closed my laptop and put it in its case. I wouldn't take my truck until I was sure another bomb wasn't inside it. Fortunately, I kept a backup car in a different underground parking lot.

"Sara? We *are* going after this guy." Connor wasn't asking.

"I'm thinking about how we'll do it, right now."

I hung up, patted the Colt 1911 in my corset holster and the Ruger LC9 in my ankle holster inside my cowboy boot. Then I locked up and left.

Once I was in my car, I called Atticus Snowden. The man could probably buy a Gulfstream jet with the money we'd already paid him. A man whose legal skills had saved our butts several times.

One of the things I liked most about him was he always came fast when we called. He made us pay for it, but he never made us wait.

CHAPTER FORTY-ONE

Sara

Based on all the research Judy and Mason got me on the man, I knew Neville Huber was not a stupid man. He'd taken a $100 million oil and gas inheritance from his daddy and turned it into — as they say — real money.

The rich contacts he'd made while working for his dad grew more influential over time. Today those men were running businesses that hired his security services, through Schlossen... or they were in the government or the military, where they signed off on huge contracts for private mercenaries through his Bangnor Group... or they brought in his rapidly growing ProCore Solutions to fix weaknesses in their I.T. systems.

Unfortunately for me, he was also a private man, who didn't attend parties or gatherings. That made it much harder to get to the man so I could kill him.

The only opening I could find was his habit of flying to the Joseph Lake Sportsman Club for a client lunch at least once a week while in Alaska.

But he could be flexible.

We quickly sent Connor up there to spend a week with Lillian, his love he met when I hired him as her bodyguard. They fly-fished, and snowmobiled, waiting for Huber to show up, which he didn't do until Connor had left.

I needed another plan.

Connor was mad as hell when my new plan didn't include him, even madder when I wouldn't tell him how I was going to do it. But I couldn't. Connor didn't know about wolf me, and I needed that ability to take my only shot at Huber.

Yes, I knew I would eventually have to tell Connor about me. I couldn't have him be the only one of the four of us who didn't know the secret. But I couldn't face it yet.

That left the whole team except me hanging out in Lupiti, Oklahoma, watched by bodyguards and a big chunk of the town's residents as well.

They'd been there for two weeks now, and I knew Connor and Judy wouldn't put up with it much longer.

I had to move now.

In my plan, Huber would be exposed for only two to three minutes, as he walked from his private lunch at the Joseph Lake Sportsman Club to his personal airplane waiting nearby. It would be daylight, in full view of many other members who were staying at the lodge or came for lunch.

There was no opportunity for stealth, so my escape afterwards was the tricky part. Assuming I was successful, the cops would question any woman who'd been at the Club — so I couldn't be seen anywhere near there.

I paid for a monthly rental on an isolated house outside of Palmer, Alaska, a small town about 70 wilderness miles due south of the Club. I was pretty sure those 70 roadless miles of nothing would be far enough away that investigators wouldn't look at people based in Palmer.

Five days ago, I'd travelled that wilderness from Palmer to the Club in wolf form. I built myself a snow bunker two miles away, in the middle of the forest, and I'd been hunkered down ever since in wolf form, waiting for Huber to show up for lunch.

Connor and Mason had both tried to talk me into taking on the heads of Schlossen and Bangnor as well. They *were* culpable, but to me they were just run-of-the-mill business crooks. I was happy to turn over anything we'd learned about them to a good reporter or the FBI.

Neville Huber was much, much worse. Somebody was going to die — either my people or him. I chose him.

When Huber wouldn't come for lunch while Connor was here, I knew I had to find someone not connected with us. Judy maintained a list of grateful former clients who wanted to help us in any way they could.

Of them, only Doug Ramsey had any money, and I needed someone wealthy enough to join the club.

Doug owned Oklahoma's most successful car dealerships. He'd started with one in Tulsa, then added Oklahoma City, and today he had six of them in the state. He was also the father of one of the girls that was rescued when we exposed a human trafficking operation. She wasn't a girl we personally rescued, which might have tied her to us, but one the FBI was able to save from the records we were able to expose.

Doug tried to give us cars, to express his gratitude. When we wouldn't accept them he offered to help us in any way he could. I'd had lunch with him a couple of times since the rescue and I liked the old coot. He was crusty and ornery enough to be a Texan — just not quite as arrogant.

Still, it's a long way from liking a man to trusting him to be an accessory to murder. Thank god for my lie-detector nose. I'm 99% accurate about whether or not someone is lying. No matter how practiced he or she is in deception, apocrine glands know when their owner is lying and they emit an acrid smell from our underarms and groin. For a practiced liar, the release is so small it takes my wolf nose to detect it.

Another lunch and evening drinking with him and his wife — giving them ample opportunity to lie — convinced me I could trust them. And they were eager to help.

Most importantly, I could think of no other way to get Huber. I needed them.

Doug joined the Joseph Lake Sportsman Club last week, and he wouldn't let me reimburse him. He and his wife then came here for vacation. They went ice-fishing right out the door in holes drilled on the lake. And took snowmobiles to well-stocked streams, some of which were still running.

Doug made a point to hang out with the guides, pumping them for info about an imaginary trip with them he was planning. His wife cultivated the chef — getting him to talk about all the special food dishes he cooked.

One day while the Ramseys were snowmobile joy riding, they discretely dropped off two bags of supplies for me. One was full of human snow clothes and the custom backpack I could wear in wolf form. The other had 40 packages of beef jerky, a communications unit and an AR-15 semi-automatic, fully loaded. With one extra magazine.

Each night I got out of the cave and looked around. Mostly I walked on snow to the edge of the forest of lodgepole pine trees, where the land had been cleared for the Club. The trees were very, very tall and narrow. I had to stay close to the trunks of them to make sure the thickness hid me.

From there, I looked out over the Club's summer patio — still covered in deep snow — to the windows of the dining room. The front of that room led out to the pier jutting into the lake. In the summer, water planes would ferry members to and from the club. In the winter, single engine props and jets landed on the thick ice covering the lake, before taxiing to the pier.

There was 50 feet between the door to the dining room and the edge of the pier, where Huber would get into a plane and be lost to me. I figured at least five people, maybe up to ten would be able to see me make my move.

But first, I would have to get from these trees to the club without raising an alarm. The layout of the club was one big, main lodge which held the lounging area plus the game, exercise and dining rooms. On the far side of it were guest cottages, spreading out around the lake, but connected by an inside hall that spared members from needing to go outside unless they wanted to. Behind the main lodge was a similar-sized but plain building which held rooms for the staff, supplies, and all the winter toys rich people might want to use.

The back building was the closest to the trees, only 50 feet. But Connor told me no guests ever went there. I couldn't pretend to be staff — there weren't that many and everyone knew them all by sight.

I also couldn't go in the main building without risking discovery.

My safest move would be to appear to come from the guest cabins, walking towards the dinning room. To get there, I'd have to cross 50 feet of empty land to the back of the rear building, travel the length of it, then walk across about 25 feet of empty land to get to the first of the guest cabins.

Then I'd have to turn and walk the entire front length of the main lodge to get to the pier. I also had to time it so I got there the same time as Huber did.

While carrying an AR-15.

Hmm.

CHAPTER FORTY-TWO

Sara

I was snoozing in my ice den, my fluffy tail covering and warming my nose, when my snow suit buzzed. My coms unit that connected me to Doug was in one of its pockets, the volume turned down as far as possible without turning it off, because — hey — wolf ears.

I uncovered the unit and used a claw to tap a click that meant "go ahead." Doug's voice said, "We have a possible for lunch today. The chef's making Beef Wellington, something he says he makes once a week or so and only for one member — because of all the prep time. He didn't say who and I didn't ask. I'll let you know if it's him when I see him."

My claw tapped an acknowledgement, and I used my teeth to put the unit back in the snowsuit. I was already prepared, so I went back to sleep.

I got an additional hour before the com beeped again. I stood on all four paws and shook my body. Then I again tapped an acknowledgement.

Doug's voice said, "He's here. Just sat down to lunch with the Governor of Alaska. He's got one bodyguard inside with him."

I tapped an acknowledgement click and then stretched out all of my body, as only a canine can. Then I sat down and started eating. I needed to leave this cave — as a human — in 15 minutes, just in case Huber was a fast eater.

Then I lay back, scrunched my eyes tight and let the pain of transformation take me. I'd laid out my clothes so I'd be naked for the shortest time possible. I didn't know if it was zero degrees or minus 20 Fahrenheit, but it really didn't matter. Either one could freeze your corneas off.

Once I was human, I packed up every trace of my existence into a duffle and left. I needed the shelter — which would be discovered — to look like an animal den. I dropped the bag, with empty beef jerky packages and water bottles — well inside the forest, far from the den. The cops would find it there. It wouldn't be a problem.

I kept the com unit in my ear. I'd wait until the last to destroy it.

When I left the pines, stepping into the open, I strolled.

I wore a black on black snowsuit that had a bright red "Prada" tag over my left breast and matching tag on a pants leg zipper. Knowing Judy, it probably cost $5,000. I matched it with a fake-fur snow hat which covered my ears and showed a few champagne blonde strands of hair. They weren't mine, but were taken from a wig and attached. I needed to look like a spoiled rich woman."

I also needed to look different. Huber and his bodyguards could recognize me on sight, unless they were stupidly incompetent. And there were cameras, whose video could later be run through facial recognition.

I had big orange ski goggles on, and icy blue contact lenses to cover my brown eyes. My zipped-up snowsuit came up over my chin to hide my jaw shape. My wolf-sized custom backpack was stashed empty inside my snowsuit.

I carried a short ski bag, designed for freestyle skis, balanced on top of one shoulder. But instead of a pair of skis inside, it held the AR-15.

I sighed in relief when I reached the back building without being spotted. My stroll continued on past it to the guest cabin wing. There

I turned ninety degrees to continue my walk, now looking as if I was coming from the cabins.

Huber had been sitting at lunch for 35-40 minutes by now. From the few pictures of him I was able to study — he didn't like cameras or the spotlight — he was a lean, gray-haired, 50-ish man who looked and dressed as if he could at any minute stop an out-of-control horse or lift a bale of hay. Even though he'd be doing it in clothes that cost more than a ranch hand made in a year.

I didn't figure Huber to take long, drink-fueled lunches.

I strolled across the front of the lodge area where Adirondack chairs faced the frozen lake.

I stopped suddenly and patted a pocket where I had placed a cell phone with nothing whatsoever on it that could identify me. I pretended it was vibrating and pulled it out, sticking it under my hat and against my ear.

Then I looked around and pretended to notice a chair. I brushed some light snow from it and sat, pretending a heated conversation. I lay the ski bag against the chair side, the open zipper facing away from windows in the lodge and very close to my hands.

I could keep this up for five minutes. Maybe ten.

Finally I heard a click in my ear. It was Doug's signal that Huber was getting up to leave.

A propeller started up on a plane waiting right next to the pier. The door to the plane opened and a mercenary dressed in white camouflage stepped out and waited by the plane. I was pretty sure he was wearing armor under the suit.

He and the pilot were two threats.

I stood up and gave a big, exasperated sigh. Then I said some heated nonsense things into the phone and put it away, shaking my head in disgust.

A large, military-looking guy — in a blazer and tie under a snow jacket— came out the dining room door of the lodge and saw the end of my act with my phone. I let my gaze pass over him as if he weren't there. A "rich bitch" would never notice the paid help.

Three threats.

I slung my ski bag over my left shoulder, balancing it with my right hand. At least I hope that's how it looked. My right hand was actually inside the bag and wrapped around the weapon's grip, with my index finger just outside the trigger guard.

Then I turned 40 degrees away from the plane and started walking towards the restaurant door. Towards the body guard in business clothes.

Huber came out behind him. He was about six feet tall, slim, and wearing a pale green polo shirt that was disappearing as he zipped up a brown leather bomber jacket. I recognized his bushy eyebrows, and I couldn't miss the smug look in his eyes and in the twist of his mouth.

Four threats.

I was relieved to see the governor had stayed in the restaurant.

Voices sounded back behind me, making my heart skip a beat — they were coming from the guest wing. Trying for casual, I looked back over my shoulder and saw a well-bundled-up couple walking our way. They looked innocent, but...

Six threats.

I was 30 feet from the bodyguard, 35 from Huber, when I turned away from the couple and looked where I was going. I made eye contact with Huber, one rich person acknowledging another, then looked past him to the restaurant.

The bodyguard in front of him was blocking about half of Huber's body.

Twenty-five feet to the bodyguard. Thirty to Huber.

Twenty feet to the bodyguard. Twenty five to Huber.

Without looking directly at him, I saw Huber slow. He looked at me, frowning. He was about to recognize me.

Action time.

My right hand lifted the ski-bag-covered AR-15 off my shoulder and my left hand moved quickly to the angled fore grip, which was supposed to prevent the weapon snagging on the ski bag. Not that I took the time to remove the bag — I intended to fire right through it.

Huber saw the threat and started to duck down low, reaching for his right boot and a likely pistol.

I continued forward and fired point blank three times into the bodyguard's chest, assuming he was wearing armor. The first was for center mass, but the other two shots tried for his arm which was crossing his chest going for an under-arm holster.

He fell back and down and I saw blood on his right forearm.

I adjusted my aim and shot Huber three times as he pulled out a Glock and managed to fire it — hitting my left shoulder. I closed and shot him in the head.

A bullet hit my back, knocking me down. The bodyguard from the plane. It was the first time I'd ever taken a bullet in an armored vest and it hurt like I'd been hit by a train.

I flipped on my back and fired at him, hitting his vest and — lucky shot — his leg.

The pilot had frozen with his torso just outside the plane, but I now saw him reach inside his jacket. I shot him twice, once in each shoulder.

Quickly I turned back to the bodyguard on the ground and shot him from 10 feet away in one leg and his other hand — which was holding a Walther PPK. I glanced over at the couple, but they were running away as fast as they could.

To my surprise, I discovered I'd used up the 30 rounds in my magazine. Where did they all go?

Do I reload? No. Time to run.

I kept the gun, just in case, but I turned and ran for the lodgepole pine trees as fast as I've ever moved in human form. Faster than the current Olympic men's gold medalist in the 100 yards.

Yes, I've timed myself and compared the numbers.

Not straight. No, I tried to zigzag. But... I wasn't doing very well at it. I couldn't miss the fact that zigzagging kept me out in the open longer than if I ran straight.

I half-assed zigzagged.

Bullets came flying after me, but the noise of them stayed back at the pier. When meant my threats stayed back there as well. The leg shots had worked.

Something more powerful than a pistol bullet slammed into my back and knocked me flat. My armored vest was earning its keep! I crawled back up and started running again.

The trees were 30 feet from me now. Zig!

Twenty feet. Zag!

Ow!

I took a bullet in my thigh and was again knocked down.

Again I got back up, this time limp-running.

It won't kill you, I told myself. It won't kill you.

Unless they get a head shot.

Shit! I'd meant to run with my head down.

It was pure luck I was still moving.

I lowered my head — better late than never. Finally I reached the edge of the pines.

Another shot hit my back, and knocked me forward.

I grabbed my customized backpack from inside my snowsuit as I ran into the forest. I ripped off my hat and gloves and threw them inside the bag. I wanted to take away anything that could have my DNA on it.

I dropped the AR-15, with the ski bag that somehow hadn't already fallen off. Quickly I unzipped my snow suit and unfastened my Kevlar vest.

I turned 90 degrees and ran to the rock outcropping I'd found on my night prowls. It would block any vision of me, for at least a couple of minutes.

As I stepped out of my boots, snowsuit and vest, my mind reached for the change to wolf. I welcomed it. Encouraged it to hurry up already.

A minute later I stood on four paws. Quickly I grabbed the remains of my socks and long underwear with my teeth and dumped them in the custom backpack with my hat and gloves. I got a fang in the hole of the zipper and closed the bag. I left any clothes that hadn't been against my skin.

I checked myself. My leg and sore ribs — all healed.

I inhaled deeply and was delighted to not smell any humans near to me. I stepped into the straps of my custom backpack, letting it hang down snug under my stomach.

I took a couple of minutes to leave paw prints all around the area, as if from a curious wolf.

Then I turned east, away from the Club and trotted away until I reached a patch of bare rocks. There I turned south, towards the town of Palmer and ran at top speed.

I was gasping for air after 20 minutes, and had to stop. I couldn't pant fast enough to cool down my over-heating body.

After a few breaths I was able to start back up, this time at an easy trot. I can run for days if I stick to around five miles per hour. I'd be back at my house outside Palmer before morning.

I heard single engine airplanes three times that afternoon. I moved closer to the trees each time, as a wolf would.

They were flying close enough to see me, but they never slowed or came back around.

Why would they? They were seeking a woman, not a wolf.

CHAPTER FORTY-THREE

Sara
Two weeks later

I was lying on one of my plastic lounge chairs, letting the 60 degree sun bake away any tiny hint of ambition. I felt as lazy as the meandering, brown Arkansas River that flowed past my house.

Skidi was asleep under the shade of a half-umbrella, her paws twitching in a dream. She must be chasing something.

My secure phone rang and I considered for a second tossing it into the river. But I'd have to exert too much energy to throw it out far enough... so I picked it up.

It was Mason. *Ha! I'd managed to block his annoying ring tone — at least for the moment.*

"Hi, Mason. You sent the incriminating packages?"

"Just finished. Everything we had on Huber — all the land he bought up and details on all the people he was blackmailing. I sent everything to the governor, heads of their State Senate and House, and to the top 16 news outlets in the state — everyone with at least 100,000 circulation. And I threw in the *New York Times*, the *Wall Street Journal*, and *USA Today*."

"Good. I hope it does some good. I had a nightmare where 100 years from now Alaska is 10 degrees warmer and a private enclave owned entirely by trillionaires. Anyone else who lives there must be an indentured servant to one of them."

"Jeez, that's dark. Maybe you need to do something fun to lighten up your nightmares."

"How's Emma?" I asked.

"She's doing better than I am. She's been researching hand prosthetics. She's narrowed it down to getting either a Taska or a Mia. You can control either of them with your mind, just like an organic hand. And they're supposed to give you 80% of normal function. And... the FBI offered her a job in their Financial Crimes Section, but she turned them down. She doesn't want to work for a boss."

"Mason," I said. "How are *you?*"

I heard a big sigh. "Every time I see her missing hand I want to dig up Felix and Neville Huber and bring them back to life so I can kill them personally."

"And...?"

"And... I'm so happy. Emma and I, well, we're together, and... she doesn't make me feel crowded or want to run away. And... it's wrong for me to be so happy. I mean, it cost everyone so much for me to be happy, but..."

"Mason — relax. Enjoy every moment of your happiness. Screw what you're "supposed" to feel. You've been through hell, both of you. You deserve a lot of happy times."

"She's been asking me a lot about our company. The kind of work we do. It's not for now, but down the road, after she's regained as much as she can... Do you think we could use a financial guru? Someone who can read a company's books and find how they're diverting money?"

"Absolutely."

"Okay, okay." He sighed. "So, enough about me. Have you talked to Bill lately?"

I inhaled. "Why would I do that?" I winced at how defensive that sounded, even to me.

"Sara." I heard an exaggerated sigh. "You're two unmarried people who have enough chemistry to burn buildings down. What's wrong with you?"

"He chose her."

I hit the "end call" button.

CHAPTER FORTY-FOUR

Sara

The next day I was sitting in my Tulsa office, bored out of my mind, hoping a new case would walk in the door right now to distract me.

My iWatch's ringtone sounded with "Strong Enough" by Cher. I'd programed Bill's phone number to it so I didn't have to look at the caller and get a jolt when I saw his name. This way I could just cover the watch with my hand the second I heard Cher and make the call go away.

Which I did. Again.

I kicked one of the legs of my desk and hit my toes harder than expected.

I was rubbing them when I heard a knock at the door. I grabbed my Colt 1911 from under my bra and held it behind my desk.

A very pregnant Native woman walked in and said, "I'm Yona Antwine. You're Sara Flores, I presume?"

Oh crap.

"What do *you* want?" I asked.

She waddled on in and eased onto one of the fancy chairs that Judy had bought for the office.

After a deep breath, she looked up at me. "The question is what do *you* want? Bill says you've been ignoring his calls."

I rolled my eyes. "Why is this your business?"

"Because I like the man." She smiled and patted her very large stomach. "Obviously."

I wanted to choke her.

She turned her eyes to my right hand. I looked and was surprised to find my fingers were drumming on the desk. I stopped.

She said, "You need the lay of the land."

I opened my mouth to suggest she get out of my office, but she said, "Shut up and listen. Then I'll go."

I expelled a breath of air and leaned back in my chair. I waved my hand airily, suggesting she say what she came here to say.

"Bill and I grew up together. We've been 'friends with benefits' since we graduated high school."

My eyes must have gotten bigger, because she added, "Except for most of last year, when you two were dancing around each other."

She lifted up from the chair and rearranged herself, apparently uncomfortable. "Look... our people, our history, our traditions... they mean everything to us. You know Bill's our priest. Do you know Eddie Fields?"

I nodded.

"He's our doctor, our shaman. My mother is an expert on healing plants, and I'm trying to become our people's historian. I'm writing our oral history for my Masters degree. I intend to expand it into a book. In fact, Bill says you lived next to Joe White Wolf in Colorado and I want to ask you about him someday."

She shook her head. "Sorry, I tend to go off on tangents. Anyway, our people need Bill's children. A boy to follow him. Maybe a girl to follow me."

She stared at me. "I was willing to try marriage. I mean, we aren't in love. Never have been. But we really *like* each other."

Suddenly she struggled to rise. "I sure hope there's a bathroom near here."

I nodded towards the office bathroom door. "Right there."

She waddled in and closed it.

I felt a stab of guilt for my bad manners, so I got up and opened the mini-fridge and put a bottle of water on the table beside her chair.

When she came out, she spotted the water and looked at me. I looked away so I didn't have to see her smile. She knew what it represented.

After she got as comfortable as she was ever going to be, she continued. "As I said, I was willing to try marriage, but I could see it wasn't going to work. He's in love with you. If we married, we would end up hating each other.

"So..." she again shifted in her chair, "we're raising these twins together. No marriage. Separate houses. Separate lives except for the kids. It'll probably be a shit storm, but we're going to try to make it work."

She stopped talking and looked at me. I think I was supposed to say something, but I had no clue what that would be.

I saw a smile grow on her face, but she squelched it. "Cat got your tongue?"

I slowly shook my head. I couldn't think of a single word to say.

She nodded, then struggled to get up. One of her hands slipped for a second and I started to rise to help her. But I caught myself.

Once on her feet she said, "Don't think he'll be free and clear. We're raising our kids jointly. I'll be dumping them on him for three days and nights every week, so I have time to do my research. If you don't watch out, he'll have you doing all the grunt work of caring for them."

I raised an eyebrow.

"He's a man. He's bound to try it."

A snort of laugher escaped me before I covered my mouth.

Her eyes crinkled.

I walked to the door and held it open for her.

She stopped in the doorway and said, "He has to spend that kind of time with them, or they won't bond with him. And he needs to bond with them, or what's the point of all this?"

As she waddled to the elevator, I called after her, "Yona?"

She turned.

"It was interesting getting to meet you."
She laughed and turned away.

CHAPTER FORTY-FIVE

Sara
Five days later

I paced my living room. Back and forth.

Skidi had tried to lick my hand, then thought better of it. She was now curled up on a chair, as far away from me as she could get and remain in the same room. Nothing on her moved, except for her eyes. They followed me. Back and forth.

I hadn't noticed much for a couple of days after Yona came to see me, but as my brain fog cleared and I started to think, well, maybe.... That's when I realized I hadn't heard from Bill.

No phone calls. No messages. No showing up at my doorstep.

He had to know Yona had come to see me. She would have told him. So what the hell?

Was it pride? Did he want me to beg?

Fat chance! Just what kind of game was he playing?

That did it. I grabbed my truck keys and locked up. The man was going to explain himself.

Fifteen minutes later, I pulled into the dirt driveway in front of his small yellow house off Bear St. It was a blue-collar home, different only in that it was hidden in some trees so it wasn't visible to any other houses. I always shivered when I saw it. It was his grandfather's house, and I remember the fear I had when I first came here. I'd wanted his grandfather to help me talk to the dead — to the man who'd turned me and then died on me.

Some of the historical records of the Lupiti said their priests could talk to the dead.

Bill's grandfather had actually raised Joe White Wolf in a ceremony that day. But Joe didn't want to talk to me, he wanted me to transform and kill the priest who, it turned out, had once stole away the woman Joe had loved.

I'd refused.

Bill's grandfather died without my involvement that night, which is when Bill first became the head priest.

I shook my head. Lots of bad and good memories here.

I looked around and saw only Bill's truck parked out front, although others could be here.

I took a big gulp of air when I reached the door. Steeling myself, I knocked.

Bill wasn't surprised. He'd probably seen me parked out front trying to talk myself into coming to his door.

"You alone?" I asked.

"Just me." He waved me in. "Some tea?"

I nodded, and he turned to the kitchen.

Damnit! He looked even more appealing than normal — and his normal was off-the-charts great. Although... his eyes looked tired, and a little bruised, and his shirt was rumpled as though he'd slept in it.

He looked like he needed a woman to make it all better.

Why the hell do we women fall for that look?

He came back with two mugs of tea and we sat on opposite chairs, sipping.

Neither of us said a word.

I don't mind quiet, but this was the most uneasy quiet I'd ever experienced.

I couldn't stand it, so I tried a joke, "So, you don't call. You don't write."

He tilted his head at me, as if to say, *"really? That's how you want to start this?"* Then he stood up suddenly, going from zero to 60, in seconds.

"Look," he said, frustration pouring off of him. "My life is pretty crazy right now. The woman I thought I was marrying tells me 'no,' then she says that I'm going to be caring for baby twins, alone, for three days out of the week. I don't know how to do that. I don't even know how to be a dad. Mine was never around — my mother and grandparents raised me."

He stared at me. "Then I think maybe a part of this is good... maybe I can support my people and have a family... and spend time with the woman I love..."

He glared at me.

"... the woman I thought I'd lost... but it turns out she won't even take my calls..."

I raised an eyebrow. "So all your complications are my fault?"

"Hell yes, they are. If you weren't around, my life would be much simpler."

We locked eyes.

I said, "But not as interesting."

He grimaced but nodded. "No, not as interesting."

He sighed and sat back down. "Sara, I'm not going to beg. If you no longer want me, then that's it. I know I can't offer you much. You deserve a man who's all yours. You deserve marriage, which I can no longer offer you. Yona and I don't need to be married, but we both agreed it won't work if we marry someone else before the kids have grown up."

I looked down and swallowed. The tea was getting cold, but I needed the ritual, so I sipped.

"Here's the thing," I said. "I've had marriage. At first I was so happy..." I felt my eyes burn, so I tightened my grip on my cup and tried to lock down the emotions. "Then I watched it sour. Every month, every year, it got worse and worse. That piece of paper, that marriage certificate, made him think he owned me. So he started controlling me — like he did his other possessions. I saw myself changing into the wife he wanted, while the real me shrank until I no longer recognized myself.

"I don't trust marriage. I promised myself I'd never let a man own me again. I can't stand the power it gives a man over a woman."

I frowned. "Maybe it does the same in reverse; gives a woman power over a man. It probably does, but I've only experienced it as power over me.

I shook my head. "I never wanted to marry you. The idea that you would want to marry was one of my biggest fears."

"What about all the time I'll be spending raising kids. How will you feel about that?"

I pursed my mouth. "It's actually one of the things I like most about you — your determination to keeping alive your traditions and heritage. If you could just say 'To hell with it' and run away with me, you wouldn't be the man I admire."

I drank more tea. "On the other hand, I'm sure it will be inconvenient as hell sometimes."

He put down his cup and stood, coming over to me. He knelt in front of me. "Sara, I'm in love with you. Are you in love with me?"

I closed my eyes and took a deep breath.

He took the cup out of my hands and put it on the side table. "Yes or no, Sara?"

"Yes."

He took my hands, stood and pulled me up.

Quickly I said, "But I'll probably screw it up."

He laughed and put his arms around me. I could feel his body shake in amusement.

"Then we'll be even. Because god knows I've already screwed it up, and probably will again."

I let myself bask in the feeling of his arms around me. It felt so warm... so right... so... homey. It felt like I was home.

Wait — home is being trapped. Smothered.

I jerked back out of his arms. "I'm not quitting my mission for you. I'm still running Last Chance Investigations."

He smiled and shook his head at me. "Of course you are."

"And I'm not going to be a nanny for your kids. Or a substitute mom. They're yours and Yona's. They can think of me as an aunt."

He smiled. "Anything else?"

"I won't be cleaning your house. And don't count on me to cook." I shuddered. "I'm a terrible cook."

"Got it," he said, his smile widening. "Don't let you cook. Sara, I've got a lot of faults, but from what you're telling me — they're not the ones your ex had. Don't judge me by him."

I nodded. "Fair enough."

So..." he said, "what *do* I get?"

"What do you get??"

He nodded. Fortunately for him, I saw his eyes crinkle.

"You get someone who's on your side. A best friend who will listen to your hopes and fears and who will keep all your secrets. Someone who will go to war for you, or just hold you — whichever you need most. Someone who wants you to be as happy as is humanly possible. Someone who loves you with all her heart."

He smiled and pulled me back into his arms. He said into my ear, "That sounds pretty good to me."

I pulled back a little to see him. "I'm a little scared."

"Me too. But, hey, how bad could we screw this up?"

I laughed. *Really* laughed. "Oh god, don't ask!"

Suddenly, he pushed back and held my shoulders. "Wait a minute. You didn't say anything about sex."

I smiled. "I thought that was understood."

He tilted his head. "You know... I've seen some werewolf movies, and... you don't turn into a wolf during sex, do you?"

I looked at him and raised an eyebrow. "I don't know. Wanna find out?"

"Oh, yes."

END

AFTERWORD

Doing research is one of the fun benefits of writing a novel. The strangest questions arise, and I get to go down rabbit holes to find answers.

For example, the abandoned Nike Hercules missile sites in Alaska. Eight of them exist and you can find pictures and site plans for them. Unfortunately for me, they were all near active military bases, so I invented a ninth site in the middle of nowhere — Test Site 9.

I also got lost for a couple of days looking at mini-submarines. There are models that only go down 30 feet, but can jump up in the air and race like speedboats. In another life, I hope to get to take one of those for a spin. There are also three-seaters that can go much, much deeper. Even though I don't have claustrophobia, I'm not planning to go down in one of those. Ever!

ABOUT THE AUTHOR

Did you ever want to be more than yourself? I always have. As a kid, I imagined I lived up in the clouds with a band of other kids. We would swoop down — because we could fly! — and rescue people in trouble. And we'd beat the crap out of their abusers.

When I got older, I became obsessed with crime and mysteries. I wanted to know how someone could track down evil doers and peel back their false faces — exposing them to the world.

The day I quit my corporate job — my dreams came true. Today I spend my time throwing my character, Sara Flores, at one criminal mastermind after another — just to see what she can do.

And... I cheated. I let her be more than herself by making her a werewolf — the only magical creature in a world otherwise just like ours. Because I wanted to see what she could do with a wolf's senses and strength. And wildness.

So join me for stories of ruthless criminals, suspicious cops, and Sara's small band of misfits fighting to save us all.

ALSO BY SUE DENVER

SERIES: SARA FLORES, WEREWOLF P.I.

BOOK 1: *Will her first case be her last?* New Private Investigator
Sara Flores is up to her werewolf snout in hired assassins and explosives
while trying to save her first client's life. [146-page novella]

BOOK 2: When a billionaire wants you dead... how do you survive? *Private Investigator Sara Flores was hired to find a woman who left her Tulsa casino job 192 days ago - and hasn't been seen since. The cops say Alaska Brown left willingly. The FBI isn't looking. And now, someone deadly is trying to kill off Sara and her team. Someone with unlimited funds. Has she the right to risk all their lives? But... how can she not? Can Sara and her 3-person team of misfits really take down a billionaire — or is this the case that gets them all killed?* [268 pgs.]

BOOK 3: Murder, blackmail, and a female werewolf running loose in Yellowstone Park. *A young woman has disappeared. She was seeking evidence her father was murdered 11 years ago... That he didn't die in a Wyoming snowstorm because he was too drugged and too stupid to find shelter. Sara races from Big Sky to the Crow Rez to Yellowstone Park, trying to find the girl before she meets her father's fate. But the man behind her kidnapping has a billion-dollar money machine to protect. Nobody's dared to cross him in 20 years — at least nobody alive to tell about it. Not the girl's dead father. Not Congress. Hell, not even the last three U.S. Presidents. What can Sara do?* [242 pgs.]

SERIES: SARA FLORES, THE EARLY YEARS

BOOK 1: *Abandoned. Nobody to show her the ropes. How will she use her new powers?* *Sara's first 8 adventures — from before she became a werewolf through her first year. See her transform herself into an avenger of the powerless and into evildoers' worst nightmare. Seven short stories and one novella.* [204 pages]

BOOK 2: *Payback is a bitch!* *Includes three novellas:* **BETRAYAL IN OKLAHOMA** *(Sara's going to save that little boy if she has to bite the heads off half the criminals in the state. Literally.),* **THE STENCH OF FEAR** *(Sara's after a man who's working with the cops. She can't stop because they're killing women), and* **AMATEUR ASSASSIN** *(Sara faces the ethical dilemma of her life. Should a man die for what he will do?)* [210 pages]

www.ingramcontent.com/pod-product-compliance
Lightning Source LLC
Chambersburg PA
CBHW061454030726
47503CB00005B/1700